STRIPPED

MEET ALANA

BOOK 1

D1707868

JEtt
GOTTESFELD

SADDLEBACK
PUBLISHING

9836

STRIPPED

Stripped
Wedding Bell Blues
Independence Day
Showdown on the Strip

SADDLEBACK
P U B L I S H I N G
www.sdlback.com

ISBN-13: 978-1-62250-768-9
ISBN-10: 1-62250-768-1
eBook: 978-1-61247-979-8

Printed in Guangzhou, China
NOR/0414/CA21400667

18 17 16 15 14   1 2 3 4 5

With gratitude, for my team at Saddleback.

MEET THE CHARACTERS

ALANA: Heiress Alana Skye, daughter of famous billionaire hotelier Steve Skye, is drop-dead gorgeous. But her life has been less than happy. And she has a difficult time living up to her father's demand for perfection.

CHALICE: Rich girl Chalice Walker is one of Alana's besties. Her ditzy, fun-loving nature masks an old soul. College is not for her because she's an artist at heart.

CORY: In the glitzy world of Vegas, Cory Philanopoulos was Alana's rock. Then he went to Stanford and everything changed. Back for the summer, rekindling a romance with Alana is not on his radar.

ELLISON: Why is Ellison Edwards working as a personal trainer in the luxurious LV Skye Hotel when he can afford any Ivy League school? And he has the brains to get accepted.

KAYLEE: No stranger to poverty and hardship, Kaylee Ryan literally falls into her dream job at the LV Skye. As Alana Skye's personal assistant, no less. Will poor girl Kaylee get along with Alana's rich besties?

REAVIS: From Texas like Kaylee, Reavis Smith is determined to make it big in Sin City. He's a street magician with a secret identity. And he's making a name for himself all over town.

ROXANNE: Supermodel Roxanne Hunter-Gibson is beauty and brains combined. She's managed to make a killing with an entrepreneurial start-up. Now she's Steve Skye's latest hot squeeze.

STEVE: Self-made man, cunning, rude (and some would say a lot worse) are some of the words used to describe hotel billionaire Steve Skye. And his crowning achievement is the luxurious LV Skye Hotel and Casino on the Las Vegas Strip.

ZOEY: Zoey Gold-Blum is the hottest rich girl in town. She knows it. And she uses it to her advantage. Deferring college for a year, she is out to keep her besties Chalice and Alana all to herself.

CHAPTER ONE

Some say that New York City is the city that never sleeps. They say wrong. The city that really never sleeps is Las Vegas, Nevada. "Sin City." "The Gambling Capital of the World." For example, just about every Vegas restaurant serves breakfast twenty-four hours a day to accommodate players who decide their best time to play blackjack is from four in the morning until noon. None of the casinos have clocks; the better to get gamblers to forget about time and focus on the riches that could come with the next spin of the slot machine or turn of the cards.

So 5:30 a.m. isn't an impossible time to be awake in Vegas. It is, however, a hell of a time for a girl who just graduated from high school to get home after a night of heavy-duty partying—particularly when "home" was the six thousand square foot penthouse at the LV Skye Hotel, located on the south side of Las Vegas Boulevard in the heart of the famous Las Vegas Strip.

The Skye was named for the famous hotelier Steve Skye. He was a man accustomed to control. And he didn't get anywhere by being nice. The girl coming through the door at that ungodly hour was his drop-dead gorgeous daughter, Alana. At almost eighteen, she was an only child.

His rags-to-riches story was known around the world. He'd dropped out of the Cornell School of Hotel Management at age twenty because he figured he'd already learned enough. His first job, way back before he changed his name from Steve Johnson to Steve Skye, was at a cheap motel in Tupelo, Mississippi.

Tupelo is known as the birthplace of Elvis Presley. Steve doubled that motel's business by convincing the owner to decorate each room in the theme of one of the rooms at Elvis's mansion in Memphis, Tennessee. He also made all of Elvis's movies available on pay-per-view on the motel televisions. He renamed the motel the Presley Palace. And he got the attached coffee shop to sell some of Elvis's favorite treats, like fried peanut butter and banana sandwiches.

Before long, the Bengali owner made Steve his partner. Four years later, they controlled over a hundred hotels and motels from coast to coast. The owner went back to India, and Steve sent him a hefty check every month.

That was the beginning of the Steve Skye story, but it was by no means the end. By the time he was thirty, Steve started the Skye family of hotels, with oh-so-chic must-stays in San Francisco, Chicago, New York, and Dallas. He was also the father of young Alana, whose home base was in New York City. She was largely raised by nannies because Daddy was always on the road visiting one of his properties or scouting locations for a new one.

Her mom, the famous fashion model Carli Warshaw, tended to be off doing fashion shoots. At least that's what she did until her infamous nervous breakdown on the runway during New York Fashion Week. After that, Carli went to a facility in Georgia for a stay that stretched from weeks to months to years. She wasn't coming to Vegas for Alana's eighteenth birthday. Alana didn't mind. When she'd seen her a few years ago, Carli could barely put together a sentence. It was scary for Alana to think that she had a dose of her mother's genes somewhere inside her.

By the time Alana finished tenth grade, Steve had built and opened the LV Skye. It was the biggest, best, classiest, hippest, most sought-after place to stay, play, gamble, and party. Here you could really have that "whatever happens in Vegas stays in Vegas" experience. Right from the get-go, the hotel had been a sell-out. It was nearly impossible to get a room. Which was no mean feat because the place had three thousand rooms that went for an average of three bills a night. Even taking into account the rooms that are giveaways, called comped, to big stars and big gamblers, the hotel took in a boatload of cash.

Alana was no math wizard, but even she could run the numbers. (3,000 x $300 = $900,000 per night / $6.3 million per week / $327.6 million per year.)

That was before a single guest paid a resort fee, ate a meal at one of the hotel's ten restaurants, visited the ultra-luxury spa, or valet parked their car. But here was the kicker: this was before the guest had even gambled away one dime. That's where the real money was made—gambling.

Before she came to Las Vegas to join dear old Dad, her father told her that he wanted her to learn the business. His goal was for her to take it over one day. To that end, he made every moment he could into a lesson in hotel management. He loved to talk about how much money there was to be made in Sin City. People who come to Las Vegas wagered $12 *billion* dollars every year. Bets on the Super Bowl accounted for upwards of $100 *million* dollars. Best of all, he explained with glee, the "house" always had an advantage when a person gambled in a Vegas casino. That edge could be anywhere from one percent to ten percent depending on the bet. If the advantage was five percent, for every thousand dollars gambled the casino was sure to win fifty dollars. The games were set up for the house to have this edge.

Once again, Alana did the math. Five percent of $12 billion dollars was $600 million dollars a year. Her father's goal was making sure a large percentage of that money was gambled away in his hotel.

Her dad had made billions from his other hotels, but the LV Skye was like a money printing press, and she and her father were the ones who benefited the most. Sure, there were investors and banks. But the fact of the matter was that her dad was richer than any of the rich guys you could name. And one day Alana would be richer than all of them too.

No wonder everyone had been nice to her when she'd started at Las Vegas Country Day School.

However, none of these things mattered when she let herself into the penthouse at 5:30 a.m. on the night before her eighteenth birthday. She'd been out all night partying with her best friends from school. Most of them were also the sons and daughters of Vegas hotel and casino elite. Some parents owned the buildings, and others owned the businesses that served the hotels and casinos. But all of them made money. Lots of money. Alana ran with a crowd that was the next generation of Las Vegas royalty. There were three main groups of kids: Big Rich, Filthy Rich, and Sick Rich. Alana was Sick Rich. She shared this category with her best friends. Zoey Gold-Blum was the daughter of the city's most famed bloggers, and Chalice Walker's dad was the most successful gaming lawyer in town. Both besties came from old East Coast money. Together, they ruled.

Alana had hoped that she could just sneak into the penthouse; that Steve would be asleep. No such luck. In fact, hotel security had called Steve the minute she'd pulled her vintage red Mustang to the valet stand. He was waiting for her in the classic early-morning pose of so many fathers pissed about their teen daughters coming in after curfew. He stood barefoot in the entry hall, wearing a white silk robe—monogrammed with the LV Skye logo— over matching sleep pants. His arms were tightly crossed. Alana opened the door to parental disgust.

"Do you know what time it is?" he boomed, probably loud enough to be heard in Los Angeles. "Do you know what day it is? Do you remember what's happening in approximately eighteen hours?"

Though there were no clocks in the casinos, Alana knew very well what time it was. Not only were there digital read-outs in all the elevators, she also had the latest beta-test iPhone sent to her from the Apple campus in Cupertino, California. Many of their executives liked to stay and play at the Skye when they needed to blow off a little steam. Meanwhile, the elevators also had high-tech video displays that listed all the doings at the resort. One of the main listings for that day was "Alana Skye's Eighteen!—Private Party, Skye in the Sky Club." She'd been out celebrating that eighteenth birthday with Zoey and Chalice. A pre-party party, as it were, with people she actually cared about. At the big party, there'd be about a thousand people and most of them would be business associates of her father. It wouldn't be an intimate experience.

"It's five thirty," she said softly. "And it's my birthday. Well, my birthday is tonight at midnight officially, but Chalice and Zoey wanted to do something extra special for me ... just us girls. They took me out."

Steve looked down at her. He was tall and thin, with thick dark hair and olive skin that favored his mother. She'd come from Lebanon. His father's family was from Northern Europe. They had been in the United States for many generations—even settling parts of Long Island, New York.

The two of them, Alana's paternal grandparents, were dead. Alana often thought her father never got over their deaths. She knew she hadn't. Her grandparents had been such a wonderful part of her life. They were always available for her to talk to, no matter what the issue. Especially when her mother was cracking up, they were there for her. Now they were gone, and they weren't coming back.

Alana pursed her lips and held back a tear. They weren't going to be able to see her eighteenth birthday either. They were always so proud of her for who she was as a person. They accepted her for who she was, not for the way she presented herself to the world.

"What are you thinking about?" Steve asked suddenly. "You're so quiet. I'm not used to it. In the casino business you have to be outgoing, Alana. It makes people want to engage with you, which makes them want to spend their money the way you want them to spend it. I always tell you that. Be outgoing. Even with me."

Ah. Another teachable moment from her dad. Alana thought about not sharing her thoughts with him. She didn't want to reopen any wounds. It was five thirty in the morning after all. Her father didn't really set a curfew for her, but there was the expectation that she'd be in bed before two.

"Nothing," she mumbled. "I should just go to bed. I'll be up and ready for the party. I promise."

She started toward her room, but Steve blocked the way. "I asked you a question. I want an answer. Remember I have the world's best bullcrap detector. To succeed in this business, you need a good bullcrap detector. There's something you don't want to tell me. Which means I will find out. So you'd better tell me."

She shook her head. "You really don't want to know."

"I really do."

Blech. She really had no choice. Her father could be relentless.

"I was thinking about Grandma. And Grandpa," she said simply. "How much I miss them. How much I wish they could be there tonight with us. That's all."

She looked up at him. She was about five eight, with a willowy figure and thick, lustrous dark hair that cascaded to the middle of her back. Her skin was pale, her eyes huge and honey brown. Tonight she wore a black cocktail dress by Michael Kors with an uneven neckline and a very high hemline. She had the legs to pull it off, and the black-and-silver Louboutins didn't hurt either. Her handbag was by Chanel. One of the advantages of being Sick Rich was that a girl could have a lot of nice things. Steve had given her a black American Express card with instructions to use it on herself. His theory was that when Alana looked good, she got photographed. And when people saw her photographs, they wanted to come to the hotel. She wasn't afraid to use the card either. She liked nice things as much as the next girl. Besides, Zoey always said that handbags lasted longer than boyfriends.

Steve blew some air between his lips and looked at her cockeyed. "It's five thirty in the morning; you're just getting home, and you're thinking about *my parents*?"

Alana nodded. She felt shy about being so honest. Maybe for once her father would be ready to have a real conversat—

"I think you should go to bed," he answered gruffly. "That's what I'm doing. Next time you come home this late, I'm not going to be so understanding. You shouldn't be thinking about your grandparents. You should be thinking about Teen Tower. We're opening soon. It's supposed to be your project."

That was it. He turned and headed back toward his wing of the penthouse. There was no sound. The penthouse had the thickest, most luxurious wall-to-wall Berber carpeting in the world. And the room was so big it took the cleaning crew an hour to vacuum it on their daily pass.

But that same carpet muffled all sound. Between the thick walls and special glass that separated the penthouse on the fifty-fifth floor from the air outside, it was as silent as a cabin deep in the woods.

That was it. No conversation. Not even an, "I miss them too." Just a gruff order to go to bed. Alana often wondered what her father dreamed of. She herself dreamed of her grandparents and of actually being able to one day run the LV Skye like her father wanted her to. The problem was that she knew she didn't have the skills to do it. She had desire, but desire without skills amounted to nothing. She often wondered if there was something else she should try to do with her life. The problem with that was her father would have a fit if she turned her back on him. He might even get angry. When truly angry, Steven Skye was dangerous.

She moved to the wall of windows that looked out on the Las Vegas Strip. In both directions, casino hotels stretched as far as the eye could see. The sun was coming up in the east, but the Strip still gleamed with the power of millions of watts of lights.

The Strip. For some, it was the setting of a miracle. For others, it was the boulevard of broken dreams. Sometimes—her father didn't know this; no one did—she liked to wash off her makeup, put her hair up in a ponytail, throw on some jeans and a ratty T-shirt, and go wander through resorts like Sam's and Circus Circus, where the clientele was far less tony than at the LV Skye. They were mostly normal people with normal lives.

Nothing about her life was normal. Not her father, not where she lived, not her friends, not her future. Who was she kidding? She'd never be able to run the hotel. She could barely do the work she needed to do on Teen Tower, her dad's latest project. It was a teen entertainment center at the hotel. If she couldn't do the work, her father would probably disown her. And then where would she be?

CHAPTER TWO

Happy birthday to me!" Alana turned to her two besties, Zoey and Chalice. "How do I look?"

Zoey gave her the up-down. "Brilliant. Every girl is going to hate you, every guy is going to want you, and Cory is going to be kicking himself for breaking up before he left for to college."

"It was a mutual thing," Alana reminded her friends. "We knew that long distance was impossible."

"Which was idiocy on your part," Zoey commented. "You could have flown up there in your dad's plane every weekend if you wanted."

"You look … poetic," Chalice decided, ignoring the conversation about ex-bf Cory Philanopoulos. "Ten on a scale of ten."

"Thanks," Alana said gratefully. For once she wasn't irritated by Chalice's annoying habit of ranking everything and everyone from zero to ten.

The previous week, Alana and her friends had flown to Los Angeles to shop for her outfit for this party. They'd met up there with the famous celebrity stylist Diana Middleton, who had picked couture for just about every famous young actress and performer over the last twenty years. Diana had taken the girls to Alexandra's Boutique on Robertson, where she'd selected what she declared was the perfect dress, shoes, and accessories for an eighteenth birthday.

The dress was by Gucci; a frothy skintight white sleeveless number with a chiffon skirt with see-through stripping at various intervals. Since she matched it with the tiniest of undergarments, there was plenty of skin for the see-through part.

Alana was glad she had privileges at the LV Skye Wonder Spa whenever she wanted; one of the hazards of having pale skin and dark hair meant that there was always something to wax.

From the hips up, the dress was form-fitting, with a dangerously low-cut V-neckline. Diana had matched it with taupe silk satin strappy sandals encrusted with crystals and a Jennifer Meyer asymmetrical silver necklace.

With her hair parted on the side like her favorite singer Kate Voegele, she knew she made quite the statement. Sexy, but not too sexy. Smart, but not too smart. Edgy, but not too edgy. Steve would approve.

If only Cory could get what I'm trying to say by wearing this outfit. Then maybe he would come back to me.

For their parts, Zoey and Chalice had decided that this was a night where Alana should be the star. They'd made it a point to dress down to let the birthday girl have the spotlight to herself.

Zoey and Chalice had already had their eighteenth birthday parties, and Alana had done the same for them—as much as Alana was capable of dressing down.

Zoey, who was tall, model-thin, and wore her blonde hair radically short, had on a nineteen twenties black flappers' dress.

Chalice, the smallest of the three friends, arguably had the best body. She was like Jessica Rabbit from Alana's favorite old movie, *Who Framed Roger Rabbit?*—the same red hair and the same eye-popping curves. Tonight she wore a red dress with a black sash tied directly below her, um, abundant chest. Tiny Chalice always wore sky-high heels, but even with heels she was barely five three.

Alana did one more spin at the 270 degree mirror in

her spacious penthouse dressing room. The object of the night, for her, was to get Cory's full attention. Though her party line was that their split had been mutual, the fact was that he'd been the one to call a halt to their relationship right before he went off to Stanford. He'd said he'd wanted to focus on schoolwork, and she'd taken him at his word.

Tonight was going to be the first time they would be in the same room since the breakup. On all his visits back home, she'd never called him, and he hadn't called her. But as the year went on, she'd missed him more and more. The good news was she'd heard no rumors of any Stanford girlfriends, boyfriends, or any other special friends. He seemed ripe for the picking.

She turned to her friends and smiled. "Operation Get Cory Back begins now. Let's do it."

The three of them padded through the penthouse to the private elevator. To get to Skye in the Sky, the premier nightclub at the LV Skye, they'd have to go down to the lobby, and then take another elevator to the rooftop nightclub. The club occupied all the space above the penthouse floors, with a twenty thousand square foot interior plus outdoor patio space on clear, Plexiglas-style patios that gave anyone stepping outside the sense that they were literally walking on air. Skye in the Sky wasn't the biggest club in Vegas—that award would definitely go to Surrender at Steve Wynn's place—but it was easily the most exclusive. Steve Skye had come up with the genius gimmick of celebrity doormen. Each night, a different A-list celeb was flown in from New York or L.A. For a couple hours they would actually work the door. This had the effect of attracting people to the club just to get up close and personal with, say, Beyoncé. Then, when Beyoncé okayed them to enter the club, the guests felt like they were at an exclusive party and happily spent lots of money.

It was up to the star to decide whether to take photographs with potential guests. Some did, some didn't.

The three girls had to cross the lobby to reach the Skye in the Sky private elevator. There were birthday party guests lined up behind a velvet rope waiting for admission. Alana recognized a few people from school and gave them a happy wave.

Security was tight, and everyone had to show both their invitation and a photo ID, plus turn over their cell phones. Alana and her friends, though, were whisked right through, cell phones in hand.

The nightclub elevator was silver and black with shimmering lights and an operator whose only job was to push the Up or Down button, but whom Alana knew had been part of the president of Taiwan's security detail. There were no other stops.

The elevator opened. And they were in.

Skye in the Sky had been named correctly. Steve had ordained that there always be a theme to its decoration. In this version the theme was deep space. All the light fixtures looked like planets or stars, and there were actual glowing constellations inserted into the high ceilings. Steve had replicas made of various NASA and Russian space capsules. These decorated the floor and provided places for people to gather and talk. The dance floor was lit from below like a spreading galaxy, while the four major bar areas were each cut out from what looked like real asteroids.

David Hilliard, a hot young deejay from Los Angeles, had been flown in to spin. He was already whipping the crowd into a frenzy. White-vested servers from the hotel's elite catering company were circulating through the crowd with drinks and hors d'oeuvres. They were all good-looking and wore white silk vests so they could be easily identified.

"Hey! Check out your cake!" Chalice exclaimed, pointing to the far end of the nightclub floor.

Alana, Chalice, and Zoey pushed through the crowd

so they could get close to the birthday cake. It stood on a special raised stand about two feet off the ground. The cake had several levels. On top were two figurines, each about two feet high. One was of Alana, wearing the same Gucci dress that she had on for the evening. And the other was of Steve, in a Tom Ford tuxedo with a custom-made shirt and black bow tie and cummerbund. To the right of the cake was a Champagne fountain that contained hundreds of gallons of Steve's private label Champagne.

"Alana! My spectacular daughter! You're here!"

Alana turned. There was her dad, wearing the same tux as the figurine on her birthday cake. For a guy in his forties, he looked pretty damn good. In fact, in drunken games of "Do Him or Don't Him" that she'd played at various parties, plenty of her high school friends said they'd do him. She always groaned, but they never changed their answer. Gross.

Steve wasn't alone. On his arm was a stunning young woman hardly ten years older than Alana. She was nearly as tall as Steve, with thick, curly dark hair and a regally long neck. She wore a knee-length silver lamé dress that conveyed the ultimate in sexiness. It would have been the easiest thing in the world for Alana to label her as a bimbo. But she knew that wouldn't be true. Her father didn't date bimbos. He didn't even hook up with bimbos. He preferred gorgeous doctors, lawyers, artists, and designers with formidable IQs.

"Remember, Alana," he'd told her in an unguarded moment. "Never get serious with a guy who can't put two sentences together. If you can't hold an intelligent conversation with him, you don't want him."

"Hi, Daddy," she said to him, feeling dutiful. He'd pulled out all the stops for this party.

"Hi, sweetheart! Happy birthday!" He hugged her, then said hello to Zoey and Chalice. "I'd like to introduce someone special to you." He turned to his date. "Roxanne Hunter-Gibson, I'd like you to meet my daughter, Alana, and her friends, Chalice and Zoey. You may know Zoey. Her moms run the *Stripped* blog."

Roxanne laughed a throaty laugh. "No, I haven't met Zoey before. But I do know her moms. Tell them Roxanne Hunter-Gibson says hello. And it's nice to finally meet you, Alana—and Chalice as well."

"Roxanne was a Ford model," Steve said. "Then she started the Vacation Channel. Sold it three years later for millions," Steve bragged. "She could retire at thirty."

"Don't age me!" Roxanne warned Steve. "That's still a few years off."

"Anyway, she just moved to Vegas. It's great to reconnect with her," Steve went on.

Reconnect, Alana thought sourly. *I can guess what kind of "reconnection" you two are making.*

Her father was famous for his three-month romances. Alana wondered how many weeks were left on this one. While they happened, though, they burned white-hot. She suspected that this was not the last she was going to see of the dazzling Roxanne Hunter-Gibson.

Roxanne reached into her bag and took out a small envelope. "Happy birthday," she told Alana.

Alana made a face. She'd specifically asked that instead of gifts, donations be made to the Children's Hospital of Las Vegas. And here was Roxanne with—

"It's a donation receipt to Children's Hospital," Roxanne explained, heading Alana off at the pass. "I thought you'd want it."

"Thank you," Alana said stiffly. "And thank you for coming."

"That's more like it!" Steve said. "I think you two are going to be great friends." He offered his arm to Roxanne. She took it. Alana noticed for the first time that she was wearing a huge diamond cuff. "Come on, my sweet. Let me introduce you to the competition from the other hotels. We all show up at each other's parties even if we hate each other's guts. Or would you rather meet Senator Reid?"

Without waiting for an answer, Steve led Roxanne into the throng.

" 'Come on, my sweet,' " Zoey imitated. She was an excellent, if brutal, mimic. " 'Let me introduce you to the competition. We all show up at each other's parties even if we hate each other's guts. Or do you want to meet Senator Reid?' And then, 'Why don't you come up to my room and be my love slave? And then we can broadcast it all over the hotel.' "

A blonde server in a simple but serviceable black dress, wearing the standard white catering vest, stepped over to Alana and her friends. She was attractive, of medium height, thin, and had a perfectly clear complexion. She carried a tray of hors d'oeuvres—caviar in starburst patterns on thinly sliced baguettes. "Hors d'oeuvres?" she asked.

"No thanks, we're dieting," Zoey told her. "But if you could bring some bourbon our way, that might be a reason to cheat for one night."

The girl smiled. "It's probably against the rules, but I'll see what I can do." She glided off in search of more willing takers. With a thousand people at the party, Alana was sure that wouldn't be hard.

"Know what?" Zoey asked. "That got me in the mood

for a real drink. Who wants to come with? I bet I can charm one of the bartenders."

Chalice raised her hand. "I'd give your chances a five. Well, maybe a seven in that dress."

Alana shook her head. "I'll pass."

"Suit yourself," Zoey told her. "We'll catch up with you." She and Chalice headed off into the crowd.

Their departure suited Alana just fine. She'd just spotted the target of Operation Get Cory Back. Cory himself. He was standing with a Latino gentleman whom Alana didn't know—Alana figured this must be one of her dad's clients. Cory had short, sandy-colored hair, intense blue eyes, a cleft in his chin, and the height and build of a water polo player, which he was. He wore black slacks and an open-collared blue shirt, so fitted it had to have been made to order.

"Okay," Alana told herself. "Be impressive."

She started toward Cory, but Cory spotted her first. His eyes grew wide. It seemed like he was about to come to her and offer birthday congratulations at the very least. But instead, he turned in the other direction and walked quickly into the crowd.

Alana was stunned. It didn't take a weatherman to know which way the wind blew. He'd come to her party but had ignored her. Then he took off.

Her knees felt weak. Her head was woozy. Her world was turning upside down. She didn't care about her party. She needed air. She needed to breathe.

On rubbery legs, she took a step toward one of the exterior doors. But she didn't get that far. A drunk guy crashed into her from behind. She lost her balance, and her legs flew out from under her as Newton's laws of motion did their unstoppable thing.

Unfortunately, she was heading right for the Champagne fountain.

CHAPTER THREE

Alana didn't end up in the bubbly. Somehow, one of the servers—a girl—got between her and the fountain. The server landed butt first in the expensive liquid. Champagne from the spouts was dripping down her hair and onto her dress. Alana, though, stayed dry. She realized that this girl had saved her from terrible embarrassment. In return, though, the girl was the subject of ridicule. A crowd gathered immediately; people thought it was hilarious. The laughter attracted more people, who joined in the mirth. Then, Alana saw someone pushing through the crowd who was not laughing at all. Her father.

"What the hell just happened here?" he yelled at the girl. "Get out of my damn fountain!"

31

As security and staff people helped the girl up, he kept up his verbal assault. "What's your name?"

"Kaylee. Kaylee Ryan."

Alana recognized her as the server who'd stopped by earlier with the caviar. For someone soaked in Champagne, she was cool and collected.

"Are you one of Alana's friends? No. You're not. You're wearing a catering vest. Do you mean to tell me that I'm paying you to wreck my party? Leave! You're fired!" Steve pointed to the door.

Alana had had enough. It was bad enough when she was the subject of her father's scorn, but this girl had gotten between her and a Champagne soak. "Daddy—"

"Leave me be, sweetheart." He swung back to Kaylee. "Go. Leave. And don't come back."

That was it. Alana couldn't take it anymore.

"Nooo!"

She stomped forward and looked up at her father, who stood by the dripping girl. "She kept me from crashing into the fountain. You should be thanking her."

"Thanking her?"

"Yeah, thanking her. I could have been hurt. You should give this girl a bonus!" She took Kaylee by the arm. "You're coming with me. Come on. You want to smell like alcohol all night?"

As the crowd watched in disbelief, Alana led the girl out of the nightclub.

Alana showed Kaylee to the guest suite in the penthouse. The bathroom had everything Kaylee would need. There was designer soap and shampoo, a plush terrycloth robe, cosmetics, a brush, lotions, and all the rest. Kaylee had beautiful shoulder-length blonde hair that would need drying, so Alana showed her where the dryer could be found. She told Kaylee she'd get her some clothes to wear for the rest of the night. Fortunately, they were about the same height and weight, so that part would be easy.

While Kaylee was in the shower, Alana went back to her room and sagged into her favorite white plush recliner. She was still upset by Cory's disappearing act. Why had he even bothered to come to her party if he wasn't going to talk to her or even wish her a happy birthday? Who does that?

She spun a million possible reasons why. He had a new girlfriend he didn't want to tell her about. He'd met someone at the party who was more interesting and more beautiful than she was. He'd heard some terrible rumor about her and didn't want to talk to her until he knew whether it was true.

She was still making up possibilities when Kaylee stepped into her room.

"Hi," she said shyly. She was wrapped up in the fluffy robe, and her shoulder-length, freshly dried hair was shiny and bright. She'd even put on some cosmetics.

Alana grinned at her. "Well, you clean up nice."

"Thanks for letting me get cleaned up," Kaylee told her. "But are you okay?"

"What do you mean?"

"Well, you were weaving up there. Did you get that bourbon your friend was asking for or something?"

Alana felt her face grow hot. "Nothing like that. I got some bad news. About a guy. Cory. Never mind."

"Huh. I got bad news about a guy today too," Kaylee confessed to her. "I'd say the thing to do is go back to your party and have a great time. Maybe even meet another guy."

"I can't do that."

"Of course you can. And if you can't, fake it."

Alana laughed. "Your name is Kaylee, right?"

"Uh-huh."

"You know, I think you're right. It's my party, and I'll cry later if I want to. So I say, let's get back up there. You're my guest now too. And I want to pay you for what you did for me tonight."

Alana kept a lot of cash on her. A girl never knew when she might want to buy something but forgot her credit card. She went to her evening bag, extracted four hundred-dollar bills, and offered them to Kaylee. The girl recoiled.

"Oh no," Kaylee protested.

"I insist."

Kaylee nodded and took the money. Then Alana found her a dress to wear. Designed by Stella McCartney, it was short, gold, and clingy, with a built-in bra. Then she got Kaylee a new pair of underwear that was still in its silk bag from the store.

"You look great," Alana told her when Kaylee had put on the clothes. And she did. As good as Zoey, Chalice, or anyone else at the party for that matter. It was hard to believe that just a short time ago, this girl had been carrying a tray of hors d'oeuvres. "What size shoe do you wear?"

"Seven."

"My size. Here. These," Alana said forcefully.

Alana had just the thing: a pair of gold-and-black leather pumps by Jimmy Choo. They cost a fortune and looked spectacular on Kaylee.

"Thanks," Kaylee said humbly. "I mean it. Can you put your digits in my phone so I can get this outfit back to you?"

"Okay," Alana said, then motioned to the door. "Ready to crash my party?"

CHAPTER FOUR

"Whoa, Alana! Who's the gorgeous stranger?"

"Hey, Alana! Looking fly!"

"Birthday girl! It's the birthday girl! And a beautiful stranger!"

Alana loved a grand entrance. When she and Kaylee stepped back into the nightclub, their arms linked, she knew that her return with the girl from the catering crew would upset her father. So she made sure to do it in the most public way possible. She took Kaylee through the club and across the dance floor like she owned it. And in a way, she did.

"How do you feel?" Alana asked Kaylee. The other girl looked spectacular in the gold dress, but Alana figured that this wasn't a girl who got out much to parties like this. After all, Kaylee was working for the hotel's catering company, which meant she'd never make a guest list. Guests and hired help did not mix.

"Kinda like Cinderella," Kaylee admitted. "I don't belong here."

"What did you tell me? Fake it till you make it, or something like that. Hey, I want you to meet my friends." She spotted Chalice and Zoey and waved for them to join her. They said the world's quickest good-bye to the people they were with, and then crossed the dance floor to Alana and Kaylee.

Zoey pointed to an invisible watch. "Nice of you to show, birthday girl. It's almost midnight. Happy birthday singing, cake, and all that jazz." Then she took in Kaylee with an up-down, up-down, up-down that Alana understood at its deepest level. One up-down from Zoey was normal. Two meant, "You're cute." Three meant, "You're hot, but don't ever think that you're hotter than me." Four? She'd never seen four. It would probably result in an immediate homicide-by-killer-stare.

Alana decided to do the intros. "Kaylee, I want you to meet my besties, Zoey and Chalice. Guys, this is Kaylee from the caterers, the girl who saved my life."

"But not the fountain," Chalice reported. "It's been wheeled out. Nice dress, Kaylee, and here's the good news.

No cell phones allowed in Skye in the Sky tonight. Just the official photographer. So you won't find yourself in an Instagram unless it's from the hotel's official feed. That dress looks great on you. Definitely a seven or an eight."

Alana saw Kaylee smile nervously.

"That's a good thing, I guess. And I was just doing my job."

"Doing it damn well," Alana declared.

"Your dad's over by the cake." Chalice was a font of information. "There's still going to be a ceremony."

"Lucky us," Zoey said sourly, then turned to Kaylee. "So, Supergirl. What's your story?"

"Excuse me?" Kaylee responded.

"Your story. Who you are, where you're from, what you're doing in Vegas, blah-blah-blah?" Zoey prompted.

"Easy, Z. It's a birthday party, not an inquisition." Alana felt protective of the new girl. Kaylee was probably only ever going to have one night like this in her life. Justice would dictate that Alana should make it a good one. Besides, it wouldn't hurt to have some good karma. Maybe Kaylee was right. Maybe she could meet a new guy right here.

Her eyes roamed around the party. Though her father's friends outnumbered hers at this point, there was still plenty of talent, but she didn't see Cory anywhere. Maybe he'd left. She made up her mind to try to meet someone new before the night was over. Even if she didn't like the guy that much, it would be a way of showing herself that what happened with Cory was not the end of life as she knew it.

"Aw," Zoey cajoled. "Come on, Supergirl—"

"Attention, attention!" the deejay's voice came over the sound system. "I understand Alana is back at the party after the, ahem, Champagne mishap. Birthday girl, welcome back!"

The crowd roared, and the deejay fed off its energy. "Can I get Alana and Steve Skye over here by the south windows? And everyone else too? We're approaching the stroke of midnight, and we've got a birthday to celebrate!"

The crowd cheered again; Alana took Kaylee's arm and stepped with her toward the south side of the club. Her friends followed. The club was ringed by floor-to-ceiling windows. The south windows looked out over Las Vegas proper. On a clear day, a person could see to Nellis Air Force Base in the east and the mountains to the south. As Alana crossed the dance floor, she spotted her dad on a small stage. The birthday cake had been moved to it. There were eighteen unlit red candles and a single blue one. When Steve saw Alana, he beamed and motioned for her to join him. A large digital clock had been set up next to the cake, counting down to midnight. She had less than two minutes until she turned eighteen.

Steve put his arm around Alana and shushed the crowd, then spoke into a handheld mic that the young deejay handed him. Alana knew her dad was a great talker. He had a way of making a roomful of people fall in love with him. He always said that if people fell in love with you, they would fall in love with what you were selling. It didn't matter if you were selling ice or dreams.

"So first of all," Steve began, "I'd like to welcome everyone to my beautiful daughter's eighteenth birthday party. It's been a great night, and we're still just getting started!"

The crowd cheered so loud that Steve had to quiet them again.

"Most of you know Alana. You know she is smart as well as beautiful, kind as well as stylish. And she's extremely, extremely good at not wrecking her own Champagne fountain."

There was laughter all around. Then the crowd quieted as Steve's voice grew more pensive.

"I'm personally thrilled that Alana is turning eighteen. As you know, eighteen is the age of majority. She's an adult now, with the power to make her own decisions and run her own life. What's most thrilling to me is that Alana wants her life to be right here at the Skye hotel chain. She has full control over the new Teen Tower here at the LV Skye. As you know, we're opening in just a few days. Alana's decisions are going to make or break Teen Tower. And this, of course, is just prep for the future."

Alana smiled outwardly and winced a little inwardly. It was true that she was supposed to be in charge of Teen Tower. But it seemed like there was a double-whammy on her work. Not only was her dad constantly looking over her shoulder, but she couldn't think of one single imaginative or creative idea she'd contributed to the project. There was supposed to be another big planning meeting the next day, this time with all the heads of staff at the hotel. Alana was dreading it.

Steve turned to Alana and spread his hands wide. "Alana, all this will be yours someday. In fact, I'm looking forward to the day when you give your old man a big retirement party right here at Skye in the Sky!"

This declaration really got the decibels up. It had been an open secret in town that Steve was grooming Alana to take over the business, but this was the first time that he'd ever said it in public. Alana had such mixed feelings about it. She'd always wanted to make her father happy. But she never thought she had the smarts to do the work. Not one single day. Even with the Teen Tower, she—

"So let's count it down!" Steve pointed to the clock. "Ten seconds till my little baby is a woman. Ten, nine, eight, seven …"

The crowd joined in without hesitation. "Six, five, four, three, two, one!"

The clock marked twelve midnight.

Omigod. I'm eighteen.

The crowd cheered. Steve handed the mic to a young woman who stepped out of the audience. When the crowd saw who it was, there were gasps and more cheering.

"And now join my good friend Alicia Keyes as she leads us in 'Happy Birthday!' "

The famous singer/songwriter bounded up onstage; the crowd sang with the superstar performer. Alana hadn't even known she was at the party.

"Happy birthday to you, happy birthday to you!"

As the song ended, Alana felt numb. The candles had been lit, and she blew them out dutifully. Then a brilliant fireworks display erupted outside the hotel in her honor. The pyrotechnics went on and on. Steve Skye never did anything halfway. When the display was over, David Hilliard started cranking the tunes again, and the party went back to full swing. Her father stepped back into the crowd, taking congratulations from friends and strangers alike. Alana didn't move. She was alone on the stage. She realized that whatever steps she'd take now, even stepping down from that stage, she'd be taking them as an adult.

It should have been thrilling. But right then, it wasn't. It was scary.

CHAPTER FIVE

Alana's iPhone sounded the next day at noon. At the same time, the butler, Mr. Clermont, tapped on her door.

"Miss Alana?" Mr. Clermont had the kind of British accent that was expected from a man in his profession, though Alana didn't know whether he'd been raised in London, England, or London, Kentucky. In fact, for all she knew, he could have been born in Vegas, and the whole accent thing could have been a total put on. Still, Mr. Clermont looked after their lives. There was no such thing as oversleeping for either her father or her when he was on duty.

"Yeah, Mr. Clermont?"

"There's breakfast on the kitchen table for you, Miss Alana. Tea or coffee, toast, soft-boiled eggs, and sliced fruit. Or I could bring it to you. Your father expects you promptly at one thirty."

Alana sighed. The meeting. Ugh. She didn't know what to be more depressed about, the meeting, or how Cory had pulled his disappearing act at her party. Both blew chunks.

"I'll come out," she called to Mr. Clermont.

"Very good," the butler said.

Alana leaned back on her pillows. She thought about Kaylee. She really liked her. And the girl had definite HGP: Hot Girl Potential. With a couple of clothes shopping trips, a visit to the LV Skye salon and spa, and a little toning in the hotel gym, Kaylee might even be hotter than Zoey. Zoey hated her on sight, and that was more confirmation of Alana's thinking because Zoey hated anyone who might be prettier than she was.

Alana was disappointed that Kaylee had slipped out of the party with the quickest of good-byes and thank-yous. Kaylee was up-front. She said what she thought, yet she still thought about what she said. Alana would have texted her, but she had foolishly not thought to get Kaylee's number when she gave Kaylee her digits. Well, at least she'd given Kaylee four hundred—

Oh no. It couldn't be. Damn.

Alana was both angry and impressed as she got out of

bed and padded across the pale pink carpet of her room in her bare feet. She'd spotted something from the bed, and if it was what she thought it was …

It was. On the ledge of a bookcase that held few books but an excellent collection of snow globes, were the four hundred-dollar bills that Alana had given to Kaylee. Kaylee had protested when Alana tried to bestow them on her but had taken them. Now it was clear that she had ultimately refused them, but not in a way that Alana would know. Not until it was too late.

Alana smiled. The girl didn't take crap from anyone. Yeah, Alana liked Kaylee. But unless Kaylee called her, she'd never talk to her again.

That was not acceptable.

Alana found her iPhone. A quick call got her to the hotel's specialty catering company, and she talked to Laura, the supervisor who'd hired Kaylee. But Laura didn't have an address or phone number for the girl. She sheepishly confessed to Alana that she'd hired Kaylee in the parking lot before the event and was going to pay her cash. Then she begged Alana not to tell the catering department head or the boss, Steve Skye. At the end of the night, though, Kaylee hadn't tracked her down to get paid, probably because of that unfortunate incident with the Champagne. She couldn't even be sure that the girl's name was actually Kaylee Ryan.

Laura went on and on, until Alana mercifully brought the call to an end. The upshot was clear. Unless "Kaylee" called her, the girl was as good as gone.

"Alana? You can go in now," her father's secretary told her. Mrs. Rogers had been Steve's secretary, personal assistant, and go-to person for almost Alana's entire life. She was as ugly as sin, as charming as a prison matron, and as efficient as an electric pencil sharpener. "They're expecting you."

It was an hour and a half later. Alana had showered, eaten, and then dressed. She knew her father frowned on jeans at business meetings, so she'd decided on a green silk blouse, black trousers, and black Lucchese cowboy boots. Hopefully, that would fend off criticism. She'd been waiting outside a conference room in the building behind the hotel that housed the company's business operations. How much money flowed through this building every day was the subject of great debate. Whether one added in Steve's considerable securities and real estate holdings around the globe, or simply totaled up the take from the hotel and casino, the number was a lot.

"Who's in the meeting?" Alana asked, her hand on the doorknob.

Mrs. Rogers waved a bony hand at her. "Everyone. Good luck. I understand you need it."

Great. That remark drained Alana of all confidence as she opened the door and started toward her seat at the large conference table ringed by men. Her father was in an imposing leather chair at the center while his various department heads were arrayed to his left and his right. Alana knew some of them. There was the casino boss, the catering boss, the entertainment boss, the physical plant boss, the electronics boss, the pool boss, the security boss ... There were so many. Men in their forties and fifties whom Alana knew were enduring the experience of working for her father in hopes of later riches. Which was not to say that Steven Skye didn't pay well. In fact, he paid great. In exchange, he expected his employees to be fiercely loyal, scrupulously honest, and do nothing but his bidding.

To Alana's surprise, there was also a woman in the room. She sat to Steve's left. It was Roxanne Hunter-Gibson, her father's latest girlfriend. She wore a sleek black pantsuit and had an iPad in front of her. This was a significant development. If Roxanne was at this meeting, she and Steve Skye had moved beyond the dating stage.

Alana couldn't remember another time when one of her father's girlfriends had sat in on a business meeting.

Then, to her shock, Roxanne spoke first. "Alana, welcome. Your dad has asked me to oversee your work on Teen Tower. You report to both of us. Think of it as an opportunity for growth."

The men around the table laughed. Alana didn't see what was funny. It was bad enough to be supervised by her father. Now her father's new girlfriend was minding her too? Her face burned at the thought of what had been discussed before she'd come into this meeting. She was sure they'd spent an hour, at least, going over all the ways that she was an idiot.

"Yes. I understand," Alana said hoarsely.

"Good," Roxanne said. "All the construction is ahead of schedule. Security is set. What we need from you are details, Alana," Roxanne told her. "What's going to make Teen Tower cool?"

Steve nodded approvingly. "Roxanne couldn't be more right. Alana, we don't expect you to hang wallpaper or put up drywall. But the creative stuff? The ideas. That's where you can shine. That's where I need you. Tell us what will attract kids around your age, and what will keep them coming back. That's how you can make your mark on this town."

"Food," Roxanne prompted. "Menu for opening day. What were you thinking, Alana?"

God. Food. Food was one of the things that her father had told her was crucial. In this day of social media, people would be doing instant reviews of Teen Tower; sharing opinions and photos. Some of those reviewers would be hoping for Teen Tower to fail.

"It always happens," her father had intoned to her more than once. "When people are at the top, those who don't have the right stuff to get there too want to see the top dogs screw up. You remember what happened when Guy Fieri opened that restaurant in Times Square? The *New York Times* killed him. Teens don't read the *Times*. But they sure read each other's tweets. Teen Tower has to be the coolest thing happening. You get me? Cool!"

"The menu?" Roxanne prompted.

Alana did what every teen did when faced with an exam question for which she did not know the answer. She winged it, trying to fill as much time with as many words as she could, even if her answer was as coherent as a dictionary reduced to confetti.

"So," she began brightly, fidgeting a little as she talked. "I've been thinking about a menu that says a few things at the same time. It needs to be hip, and it needs to be young, and it also needs to be international because we're going to have visitors from all over the world at Teen Tower, and we don't want to be accused of being insensitive. It also has to be a menu that's easily prepared because we're going to have so many people—"

"Stop." Roxanne put up a hand. "Stop with the snow job."

"It's not a snow job!" Alana defended herself.

Her father jumped in. "Come on, Alana. You just told us absolutely nothing. Except that you have no idea what you're doing. You know how many meals we prepare at the hotel on an average day? Thirty thousand. We've done banquets for five thousand people. Three or four thousand meals aren't going to bother us.

"As for the cultural insensitivity nonsense, this isn't a model United Nations. This is the Teen Tower at the LV Skye. People come to us for the experience that we can give them and the dreams we can make happen, not for a weak version of what they can eat at home. People can eat *oogali* in Tanzania and Vegemite in Australia any day of the week. We have to give them something they won't forget. Am I understood?"

"Yes, sir," Alana said weakly.

Steve stood and folded his arms. "Here's what you need to do. Birthday's over now. You're an adult. Get to work like one. Think about how you're going to make

Teen Tower great. Starting with the menu for opening day. Report back to Roxanne and me. We'll meet again tomorrow. Are we understood?"

Alana nodded weakly. Yeah. She understood. The problem was she didn't think she could deliver. Nor did she know what would happen when she failed to deliver. But it wasn't something she was looking forward to seeing.

She had to make this Teen Tower thing work. She just had to.

CHAPTER SIX

She called.

Alana was working out in the main hotel gym when her iPhone rang with an unfamiliar number from a Los Angeles area code. She didn't answer—she didn't answer her phone as a rule. Her friends texted; only strangers called. But the person left a message. Alana waited until she was done on the Stairmaster before she listened in.

"Hi, Alana. It's me, Kaylee. From last night. Anyway, I've got your dress and shoes, and I want to bring them back to you. Or maybe—" Kaylee seemed to hesitate, like she was thinking about something. "Maybe I can drop it at the front desk for you. Let me know. Thanks for everything. Bye."

That was it, but it was all that Alana needed. She had

Kaylee's digits, and it felt strangely like winning a big hand at the poker table. She went to the luxurious gym lounge and texted Kaylee, hearing back almost immediately. Five minutes later, they'd made plans for Alana to take her to dinner at the hotel. Strangely, Kaylee didn't want to get picked up. Most people jumped at the chance to have a limo pick them up. Instead, she said she'd arrive on her own.

She did, however, ask about what she should wear. Alana was impressed that Kaylee wanted to make sure she was dressed appropriately and didn't embarrass herself or Alana—again. Fortunately, Alana had sent Kaylee's dress to the hotel laundry service; it had come back dry-cleaned and pressed before noon. The dress was by some designer Alana had never heard of. A little research on her iPhone revealed that it was a private label for Target stores. Zoey would have scoffed, but that fact made Alana smile. For sure, Kaylee would never have dinner at any restaurant like the one where Alana was going to take her.

Whenever Alana went into one of the ten restaurants inside the LV Skye, she was given the best table. That is, the table reserved for her dad. All the restaurants were fine. But the finest of all was Mondrian. Vegas had a lot of spectacular restaurants. There was Joël Robuchon at the MGM Grand and Guy Savoy at Caesars Palace. Up the

Strip, the Bellagio had a place called Picasso, a nouvelle cuisine spot that featured tens of millions of dollars worth of Pablo Picasso's art on the walls.

At Mondrian, Steve Skye went one better. Not only did Mondrian have one of the world's finest collections of artwork by the Dutch impressionist painter Piet Mondrian, it also had an actual artist's studio.

Every six months, one of the world's top painters or sculptors was invited to live, eat, and play at the LV Skye free of charge. In exchange, they would become the artist in residence at the Mondrian's art studio. Few turned down the invitation because the studio was gloriously large, they were handsomely paid, and Steve Skye made sure that their every need was taken care of.

The most recent artist in residence had been Damien Hurst. In another week, Jeff Koons would be in the studio. Naturally, art lovers came from all over the world for a chance to watch a modern master at work. That they could do it while dining on the finest organic beef, line-caught California striped bass flown in from San Francisco, or non-GMO grain-fed squab, plus vegetables from the Mondrian greenhouses outside of town, made the experience even more inviting.

Alana knew that most people were dazzled by Mondrian. The décor were done in themes of muted blue, the floor in the geometric pattern of the artist's famous painting *Broadway Boogie-Woogie*, and the atmosphere was calm but formal. As she sat across from Kaylee at the prime table just outside the art studio, she could tell that Kaylee was no exception to the rule.

Kaylee arrived right on time wearing jeans and a black sweater. She was carrying Alana's dress and shoes. Alana had brought her upstairs so she could change into her black dress from last night. Then they'd come down to the restaurant and been seated at Steve Skye's personal table just outside the studio.

She'd ordered for them, with Kaylee's permission. She didn't want Kaylee to feel any more uncomfortable than she probably was. Alana was certain that Kaylee had never eaten in a place as nice as this one, and she wanted the girl to have a good experience. Who knew when she'd get to do it again?

"What do you think?" Alana asked when they'd finished the appetizers and moved on to the main course. She'd dressed simply in black pants and a sleeveless black-silk blouse, not wanting to be too chi-chi in the face of Kaylee's simple dress.

Kaylee was halfway through her fish. "I think this is the best thing I've ever tasted."

"I love that you say that," Alana commented. "You'd

be surprised how many of my friends are totally jaded about eating here. Like, they'd rather go to In-N-Out."

Alana thought of Zoey and Chalice. Like Alana, they got to eat in great places every night too. Chalice's father was the lawyer for most of the big casinos in town, which made him one of the richest men in Vegas. As for Zoey, no one wanted to make Zoey pay for any meal for fear her mothers would wreck them. Clothes, cars, food—that girl got an astonishing amount of comps.

"Are you talking about those girls I met at your party? Because if they want In-N-Out instead of this, maybe you need some new friends," Kaylee joked.

"Maybe that's why you're having dinner with me."

"I don't think they're going to be too happy if they hear about it. Zoey was all up in my business."

Alana waved a hand. "She's a piece of work. But if she's on your side? She's like a lioness. Don't worry, if we start to hang with each other, I'll work on her."

"Thanks," Kaylee told her.

"Oh!" Alana exclaimed. "I knew there was something I was supposed to tell you. You met a guy at the party, right?"

Kaylee nodded. "Yeah."

"He asked me about you. Ellison, right?"

"Yeah. He did? Really?"

57

Alana nodded and took a bite of scallop. She was always trying to lose five pounds. Not that she needed to, but she always tried to keep up with Zoey. But this meal was too good not to eat.

"Yep. He just came on staff at the hotel. He's a personal trainer in the hotel gym. Trains my dad, actually. He found me today and asked if I had your number."

"What'd you say?"

"The truth. At the time, I didn't. I could tell him now that I do. If you want," Alana added.

"He's cool," Kaylee told her. "You should let him ask you out. I thought you were the one who needed a new guy."

Alana made a face. "He's interested in you, Kaylee." She hesitated. Could she confide in this girl? She decided to take the chance. "Look. There's a problem with every guy and me. I don't know if they want to be with me for me, or for what my dad might be able to do for them."

Kaylee nodded sympathetically. "That can't be easy."

"It isn't!" Alana was grateful that Kaylee understood.

"What about that Cory guy? You don't seem worried about him."

"I'm not. His dad runs a hedge fund. He's filthy rich too."

Kaylee took a few bites of her sea bass. She seemed

intent on finishing every bite. "There's only one thing wrong about what you're saying."

"What's that?"

"You told me last night you don't want anything to do with Cory ever again."

Both girls laughed.

"I think you need to talk to him and find out where he stands," Kaylee counseled. "If you're still interested in him, that is."

"That would be a hard conversation after last night," Alana declared.

Kaylee shrugged. "Sometimes you gotta do hard stuff."

"Good advice."

"I know."

They ate in companionable silence for a while. Then dessert was served—a charlotte russe for Alana and a dish of three kinds of homemade ice cream for Kaylee.

"You know, there might be something else you can help me with," Alana ventured. It was a crazy idea, but this girl was so practical ...

"What's that?" Kaylee asked, then took a bite of one of the ice creams—the coconut. Her little squeal of delight said that she liked it a lot. Alana grinned at Kaylee's happiness. She didn't know very much about her, but there was time for that. In the meantime, Kaylee had bailed her out of one crisis. Maybe she could help with another.

"Well, I'm in charge of Teen Tower," she began.

Kaylee nodded and spooned another scoop of ice cream—this one was passion fruit. "Yeah. Your dad talked about that at your party. Like, how one day you're gonna be him."

"I'm sure that's what he's hoping," Alana confessed. "But the thing is, I'm pretty clueless about a lot of stuff. I'm just not an idea girl. Like, I'm supposed to come up with some great menu for opening day, but I can't think of anything we can serve that would be different and great. It would be a good idea if I could come up with some decent entertainment for opening day too."

Kaylee finished the guava ice cream before she spoke. "Well, I guess your problem is this is a town where you can get everything, right?"

"Right!" Alana agreed. "Take food. Every hotel has a buffet. Ours is the biggest and the best, of course. You want something you never ate before but always wanted to? Come to the Skye buffet. In fact, that's how we advertise it."

"Of course. Which is why maybe you're thinking about it the wrong way," Kaylee observed.

"What do you mean?"

One of Mondrian's blue-clad waiters brought over a couple of espressos; Kaylee waited for him to put them down before she spoke. "Well, I'm thinking that if I were coming to Teen Tower, I wouldn't want what I could get at the buffet. You said your friends like In-N-Out. Maybe they're on to something. I'd want the best teen food ever made. The best pizza. The best hot dogs. The best burgers. The best spaghetti. The best tacos. Like, the ultimate in fast food, but still food that parents could feel good about their kids pigging out on. You know what I mean?"

Alana stirred. This actually made some sense. If she were an average teen from the boonies who was coming to Teen Tower, that's what she'd want. "You mean, like McDonald's if it was healthy?"

"Not veggie burgers or tofu burgers or that kind of stuff. That's crap. No kid wants that. I don't. But what if the burgers were made from the best beef in the world? With home-baked buns? And homemade ketchup and mayo? And what if pizza got baked with the best cheese and the best sausage or the best pineapple flown in from Hawaii? What if Doritos Locos Tacos were good to eat *and* good for you?"

"I love what you're saying!" Alana exclaimed. This was the first decent idea she'd heard in weeks. "I'm gonna do it."

Kaylee grinned. "Glad that's settled." She sipped her espresso and made a face. "Yikes. That tastes like Rio Grande mud."

"It's espresso coffee. You never had it?" Alana raised her eyebrows in disbelief.

Kaylee shook her head. "Nope. And I'm not gonna start now," she said, pushing the tiny cup away. "So, you wanna hear what I think about entertainment?"

"Sure!" If Kaylee had as good ideas for fun as she did for food, Alana would be all over whatever she had to say.

"Well, there's going to be a pool there, right?"

"Uh-huh."

"With diving boards, right?"

"Definitely," Alana confirmed. "It's actually like a small water park."

"Well, why don't you get the United States Olympic diving team to put on a show? Those guys are hot. And get some huge entertainers to play sets. In fact, you could carry this past opening day. Do a mystery performance every day at three o'clock. You can afford it. Maybe make a deal to broadcast it live. Like on MTV or something. Or stream it."

Alana's jaw hung slightly open because Kaylee had tossed these ideas off as easily as she would make a grocery list of basic staples. Each idea was better than the next.

The one about the live show being streamed or a possible broadcast deal with MTV? That was genius. Imagine the publicity for Teen Tower. It was just as brilliant a concept as the food idea.

"You're very good at this," Alana told her.

"Thanks. I'm just glad to be helpful. It can be my thanks for this great dinner."

"So, what really brings you to town?"

Kaylee seemed to squirm. "Like I said, it's my gap year …"

Alana sensed Kaylee's discomfort and tried to figure out what was behind it. The more she thought about it, as smart as Kaylee was, the more she figured that Kaylee was a rebel girl. Probably she had parents who expected her to go to college, and she was out running around for a year breaking their hearts. She had no money, which was why she had been willing to work for the hotel's catering service. Her parents had probably cut her off. It made Alana think of that movie, *Into the Wild*, where the smart college kid ran away from his parents to bum around the country and go to Alaska.

"Okay. I get it. You don't want anyone to know you're in Vegas," she declared knowingly. "Is that it?"

"Something like that. Yeah."

"Well, no problem, then. You saved me last night from

the Champagne fountain, and then you save me tonight from my dad. I can't wait for him to hear some of your ideas. I've got your back. If you're gonna be my friend, I'll cover for you." Alana leaned forward. "Is there anything I can do for you to repay you a little? You wouldn't take my money. But I want to do something. I need to do something. All you have to do is tell me."

Kaylee seemed to hesitate. Then she sighed. "Okay. But I'm only asking because you want me to. Is there a chance I can get a job at the hotel? And if I can, are there also jobs for two of my friends?"

A half-hour later, the elevator opened into Alana's penthouse. With dinner finished, Alana brought Kaylee upstairs. She wanted to show her new friend that she could help her, and help her right away. Three jobs at the LV Skye? That should be a snap.

"If my dad's here, I'll ask him. And if he's not here, I'll ask him another time," Alana said. She called out, "Dad? Dad! You around?"

Steve wasn't home. But Mr. Clermont most certainly was. He seemed to need very little sleep.

"Your father's having drinks with the governor. And with Roxanne," he reported.

STRIPPED

"Perfect. The She-Devil of Las Vegas," Alana muttered under her breath.

"Excuse me?" Mr. Clermont asked.

"Nothing. Anyway, I have to talk to him. It's important." She looked over at Kaylee to underscore that she was looking out for her. Kaylee smiled with gratitude. "When's he coming home?"

"Soon. But from what I heard?" the butler said. "I wouldn't say anything to him about anything until you talk about Teen Tower strategy with him and Roxanne. After today's meeting, I understand you have some ground to make up, as they say."

Alana thought of all the ideas Kaylee had provided at dinner. "Actually, Mr. Clermont, I'm fine to talk with him tonight. Even both of them. When he gets home, send him to my room. I'll be in there with Kaylee. Come on, Kaylee."

While she'd been talking with Mr. Clermont, Alana thought of something she could do for Kaylee immediately. As they crossed through the penthouse, Kaylee seemed to be taking in every nook and cranny of the place.

"You need a new cleaning person," Kaylee declared when they reached Alana's room.

"What? We've got the best crew in the hotel in here every day."

65

"Well, they could use a refresher course."

"Come on," Alana scoffed. "They're great."

"Not so much. Whoever vacuumed the carpet had one section going the wrong way. Two of your paintings have smudged frames. There's a bulb out in the entryway chandelier, and one of your doorknobs needs polishing. Look."

Kaylee pointed to the doorknobs on the double doors leading to Alana's bedroom. Sure enough, the French brass was dull on one side. Alana compared it to the other side, which gleamed.

Wow. Kaylee was right. The crew could use a good talking-to. Hard to believe Mr. Clermont had missed these things.

"I'll talk to my dad," Alana said quietly.

"My friend Jamila and I are really good cleaners," Kaylee offered.

Alana nodded. "I'll remember that. But I wanted to talk to you about something else."

"Yeah?"

"You needed to wear the same dress you wore last night. Which tells me that you don't have a lot of clothes." She thought of the teen guy in *Into the Wild*, who left home with very few clothes. "Probably you did it on purpose. But if you're staying in town, you'll need clothes, and I know you don't have a lot of money. I want to go through my closet with you. We're the same size, and I have a lot of stuff I've only worn once. I want to give them to you."

Kaylee seemed to bristle. "No, thank you. I don't need any of your clothes."

"Hey, no offense. But that black dress is going to fall apart if you wear it every day."

"No, thanks."

Alana thought Kaylee was being too proud. It wasn't like those once-worn clothes in her closet were doing any good for anyone. "How about I take you shopping for comps?"

"Comps? Isn't that what the hotels give gamblers? So they can stay and eat for free while they play?"

"That's gambling comps. What I'm talking about is store comps. Do you think I always pay for clothes?"

Kaylee's eyes grew wide. "You get free clothes?"

"Sure. Lots of stores want to be on my dad's good side. Or maybe they want a picture of me with the owner or something. They give me clothes. They'll give you clothes too, if I tell them to."

"That's … that's crazy."

"That's how it is," Alana declared.

"What will I need to wear if I work here?" Kaylee asked.

"A lot depends on where we put you. I'm going to ask my dad if you can work on the penthouse cleaning crew. Because—"

Suddenly, the door opened and Steve strode in. He looked very unhappy.

"I heard that, Alana," he boomed. "I'm telling you right now: that girl is working in this penthouse over my dead body!"

CHAPTER SEVEN

Five minutes later, Alana sat across from her father in his private library. She felt bad asking Kaylee to wait in her room alone while she talked to her father. But she was proud of herself for insisting that the conversation be private. As she had the night before, Kaylee handled the situation with grace. In fact, before Alana and Steve departed, Kaylee even reintroduced herself to Alana's dad and thanked him for dinner.

"I had dinner with you?" he asked dubiously.

"I ate with Alana here at the hotel. I figure you were treating us."

Alana saw her dad stare at Kaylee in disbelief. Then, something like respect crossed his face. "Well, that's a refreshing attitude."

"Come on, Dad," Alana had urged. "Let's go. I don't want to leave Kaylee alone for long."

"Oh, she won't be alone. Mr. Clermont will stand watch outside your door," Steve declared.

The message was clear. Kaylee was not to wander around the penthouse unsupervised.

"I'll be fine," Kaylee assured her. "I'll just watch some videos on my phone."

Alana had never seen her dad read a book. He was too restless for reading. That fact did not stop him from having an excellent private library right in the penthouse. It was designed by a librarian from some British historical society. It had a real fireplace, shelves full of the old encyclopedias that Steve collected, and a couple of plush leather chairs that flanked an onyx chess set. Alana and Steve occupied those chairs. Steve began the conversation. Ninety-nine percent of the time, Steve began the conversation.

"You had dinner with the girl who saved you from falling into the Champagne fountain, and now you want her to work in our home. Do you even know her name?"

"Of course I know her name. Kaylee Ryan."

"Did you check ID?"

Alana dead-eyed her father without saying a word. To his credit, he actually backed off. "Hey. I'm just looking out for you. I've only got one daughter. When people want something, they can say all kinds of things that aren't true."

"Well, she's an amazing girl. Actually, she's like a muse to me," Alana maintained, exaggerating more than a little for the benefit of her dad. "We were talking about Teen Tower. It was the strangest thing. The more we talked, the more I thought of all these unbelievably great, creative ideas. I couldn't wait to talk to you about them either."

At the phrase "unbelievably great, creative ideas," Steve sat back thoughtfully in his chair. Alana knew that he wasn't used to hearing enthusiasm from her when it came to the hotel business. At the same time, enthusiasm was the one thing that he really wanted from her. That and genius. She realized that tonight he could be getting a dose of both.

At the phrase "I couldn't wait to talk to you," his eyes widened to intergalactic Frisbees. She knew he'd never heard that phrase from her before. Not once.

He smiled wryly. "Well then. Why don't you tell me about these 'unbelievably great, creative ideas,' and we'll see how unbelievable and creative and great they really are. Where'd you guys eat, anyway? Chinese? Thai? Italian?"

"Mondrian," Alana reported.

Steve barked a laugh. "Mondrian. Taking her right to

the top. Did you tell her she could pose for a Jeff Koons painting in a week or two? Okay. All kidding aside. Bring 'em on."

Alana took a deep breath. Her father could be a harsh critic. On the other hand, she could see how hopeful he was that this would be the moment Alana would break out of her shell and display the promise and the shrewdness he was certain was in her DNA. Not from her crazy mother. God, no. From him.

"Okay. So I was going to report all this to you and Roxanne tomorrow, but I can't wait." Alana uncrossed her legs and leaned toward her dad. "Kaylee and I were talking about the food at Teen Tower, and I got this great concept for a menu not just for opening day, but for the next few months—until we decide to revamp."

With that as her opening, she laid out Kaylee's idea about top-of-the-line, all-premium ingredients, teen-ager friendly food options. She gave as much detail as she could, even expanding on what they'd talked about at dinner. With Kaylee's idea in her head, she had plenty of room to riff. It was like all she needed was Kaylee's core idea, and then she was off and running. It was like choosing accessories to go with a gown by Dior.

"So," she concluded, "we would have Kobe beef burgers and mac and cheese made from artisanal ingredients.

Something like Taco Bell's Doritos Locos Tacos, but with handmade cheesy taco shells, and fresh yellowtail for the fish tacos, and beef from Montana grass-fed ranges for everything else. There'd be pizza like Juliana's in New York, but with even better cheese and sausage that we'd grind right here. We'd bake it in a brick oven like the ones they had in Italy before everything got mass produced— maybe get a *pizzaiolo*. We could import the bricks for the ovens from Naples. What do you think, Dad? I mean it; we could have our own ranch and fishmonger so we're confident of where everything comes from."

By way of answer, her father stood. Then he walked over to one of the old wooden globes in the library and gave it an idle spin. Alana couldn't see his face. She had no idea what he was thinking. She got the answer when he finally turned around. Her father didn't have to say a word. Instead, his face glistened with tears.

"My God, Alana," he whispered. "You've got it. I always thought you had it in you, but I never saw it. You have it. You have it. You have it. You can do this!"

With a little whoop, he practically danced across the library carpet, swept Alana up in his arms, and whirled her around. Alana was stunned. She couldn't remember the last time she'd seen her father cry. In fact, the only emotions she generally saw from him were satisfaction, disappointment, or anger. And the satisfaction was rarely directed at her. She didn't remember him crying at either of her grandparents' funerals, nor when Alana's mother was hospitalized the first time. He hadn't shed a single tear of nostalgia or pride at her eighteenth birthday. But he was crying now. And laughing. And still spinning her around.

"You have it. You have it!"

For the briefest instant, she thought about telling him the truth. That it wasn't her who'd come up with these concepts. That even after eighteen years beside the great Steve Skye, she hadn't learned the hotel business by osmosis. That the mystery girl now chilling in her room was the genius. Kaylee Ryan. The one who'd saved her from embarrassment at her birthday party. The one who was a little vague about her past.

Alana decided to keep her mouth shut. Her father wouldn't believe it anyway, and it was great having him love her like this. It was perfect. Kaylee wanted to work at the hotel. All Alana had to do to maintain her ruse was convince her father to put Kaylee on the payroll. Kaylee could be her private muse. She said she needed a job. Hell, she'd get jobs for Kaylee's friends if that's what it would take to convince her. Then Kaylee would owe her. It would be the perfect relationship. Each had something to give to the other, and each needed something from the other. It could go on forever. At some point, they'd share some version of the truth with her dad. When Teen Tower was a huge hit, he wouldn't care.

Steve finally put her down to the floor. Then he rubbed his eyes. When he spoke, it was from his heart in a way that Alana had never heard before.

"You have to understand, Alana." His voice was husky. "You're all I got. If you don't take this place over, it's going to end up in the hands of a bunch of Harvard Business School bean counters, who don't have any idea what we're really selling, and they'll turn it into just another Vegas joint—a cash cow that they'll milk until all the milk is gone. You know what we're selling, right?"

"Dreams," Alana said obediently. She'd heard her father say this a hundred times.

"That's right. We're selling dreams. This whole city is selling dreams, but no one does it better than we do." Steve spread his arms wide. "People dream of money, of sex, of glitz, of entertainment, of a world that's one big playground and they're the king of the merry-go-round hill. That's what we give them." He moved closer to Alana. "What's the other one?"

"What?"

"The other idea. You said you had another great idea. What is it?"

"Ah!" Alana exclaimed. "Well, two ideas really. About opening day entertainment. I want to bring in the United States Olympic diving team to perform an exhibition in the pool. The other idea is to have a three o'clock concert out on the deck. Every single day. Broadcast live on MTV. You know, *Live from the Skye TT*."

Steve's eyes grew wide. "I love it! The diving team? Genius. And I love the TT concert thing too. We'll call MTV tomorrow. I know all those people at Paramount. Maybe we'll do the first one as a special and build from there."

"You have to let Kaylee and me choose the bands," Alana told him. Music was actually something she knew about. The wrong band could send totally the wrong message.

"Kaylee? What does she—" Steve hesitated. "Done," he said.

"Maybe we can even have an MTV studio here at the hotel," Alana ventured.

"Yes!" Steve punched the air. "Who would have thought? My Alana turns eighteen and she turns into ... well, the next Steve Skye. I'm proud of you, sweetheart. You've found your calling. Most people never do."

Once again, her father had it all wrong. Once again, Alana didn't correct him. That wasn't what she needed to do. What she needed to do was get Kaylee on the hotel payroll and fast. There was also the matter of Kaylee's two friends, but they were less important. First things first.

"So can you hire Kaylee?" she asked.

"To do what? Clean rooms?"

"No." Alana cleared her throat. "I want her to be my personal assistant."

"Done," Steve told her. "Take her to personnel in the morning."

"Great!" Alana exclaimed. "That's perfect."

Alana stood. She wanted to get back to Kaylee and share the amazing news. "I'm so excited, Daddy. In fact, I can't wait to get to work tomorrow."

"Did I just hear my daughter say, 'I can't wait to get to work tomorrow?' What did I say we were selling here? Dreams? Because I'm wondering if I'm dreaming right now." Again, her father had that huge grin on his face. Alana loved to see it there. She wished she could keep it there all the time.

"I want to go tell her now," Alana declared.

Steve pointed to the door. "I'm going to sit here and think about my wonderful daughter. Go."

Steve didn't have to tell her twice. Alana practically flew out the door.

CHAPTER EIGHT

Whether her feet actually touched the carpet as she ran from the library back to her bedroom was debatable. She blew past Mr. Clermont, still standing at the entryway to her wing of the penthouse, and opened the door to her room. Kaylee was sitting on the floor, calmly looking at something on her phone.

"Hey," she said. "I've been reading about Vegas history. Did you know that the first hotel—"

"Stop," Alana ordered. "Don't talk. Just listen. I come with big news."

"Good big news or bad big news?"

Alana grinned from ear to ear. "The best news possible. You've got yourself a job."

Kaylee made two fists and pumped the air. "Yes! Yes,

yes, yes!" Then she turned to her. "In housekeeping, right? Where do I get my uniform?"

Alana laughed. "Housekeeping? Housekeeping?" She howled with laughter. "Housekeeping."

"What's so funny?" Kaylee asked. "I'd love to do housekeeping."

Alana went to her and took both her hands. "Kaylee. You're way too good for housekeeping. I'll meet you at the hotel personnel office at eight in the morning. We'll get started right after that. I'll give you the grand tour. You're going to be my personal assistant."

Kaylee's voice went flat. "That's crazy."

"Crazy, maybe. But true. Congratulations. And welcome to Vegas," Alana declared.

"Um … what does a personal assistant do?" Kaylee asked.

"We're gonna figure that out together." Alana let go of Kaylee's hands and moved to her bed. She really did look forward to starting work tomorrow.

Kaylee looked at her. "Can I ask you one more thing?"

"If it's about money, I don't know yet," Alana said. "That's kind of up to my dad."

Kaylee shook her head. "It's not about money. It's about something else."

"Sure, anything," Alana told her. "You've got me in

an accommodating mood considering that you've saved
my butt over and over again. And if it's about Zoey and
Chalice, don't worry about them. They'll be fine. And
don't worry about those two friends of yours who want
to work here. I haven't forgotten about them. Now, go get
some rest. You've got a big day tomorrow. We both do.
Where do you live anyway?"

Kaylee made a vague gesture. "Out toward UNLV."

"Well, that's not far. If you want to take the hotel limo,
just go to the concierge desk and have them call up to me.
And, Kaylee?"

"Yeah?"

"You are my official lifesaver. I'll never forget it. Come
on, I'll walk you out."

She went with Kaylee to the elevator and waved as the
doors closed. Then she stood there for a few moments.
She felt great. Her father was right. Vegas was a city of
dreams, and she'd just made her dream and Kaylee's
dream come true.

CHAPTER NINE

Alana was not going to let anything get in the way of her secret weapon being hired at the hotel. She met Kaylee in the morning for breakfast, and then escorted her to the hotel personnel office. She even walked her through the paperwork. Then she waited with Kaylee for a face-to-face with the head of hotel personnel. This last part wasn't usual for low-level new hires, but Alana wanted to impress her new employee.

"What about housing?" Kaylee asked nonchalantly. "I heard some people who work here get apartments."

"Where'd you hear that?"

"I read it online somewhere."

Alana grinned. "Good. Keep reading. Do you check

Stripped every morning when you wake up? Zoey's moms' blog?"

Kaylee shook her head. "Should I?"

"If you're working with me? Yeah, you should," Alana declared. "That blog can make us or break us. As well as everyone else in town."

"So what about the housing?" Kaylee circled back.

Alana wrinkled her nose. She was curious why Kaylee was pressing this. Then, joking, she said, "Why? Don't you have a place to live?"

"Of course I have a place to live," Kaylee answered instantly. "It's just that ... well, it seemed cool."

"It's not so great," Alana told her. "Four people to an apartment, and you don't choose your roommates. It's assigned. Two bedrooms, little kitchen, little living room, and a reduced rent gets deducted from your paycheck. I guess if a person was homeless it would be okay. Thank God you're not homeless."

"That's for sure," Kaylee told her.

The head of personnel's office door opened, and a crisp middle-aged woman in a white pantsuit came out. Alana stood. So did Kaylee.

"Hi, Alana, it's great to see you," the woman greeted Alana warmly.

"Hi, Sandra," Alana greeted her. "Sandra, this is Kaylee

Ryan, my new assistant. Kaylee, this is Sandra Loggins, head of personnel. All good, Sandra?"

Sandra nodded. "All good." She looked over at Kaylee. "We're starting you on salary at seven fifty a week. Bring me a voided check if you want direct deposit, or we'll mail a check out to you. We'll talk benefits, etcetera, after ninety days; that's standard. Welcome aboard. Good luck."

Alana watched Sandra stretch out a hand to Kaylee, who stood in shock even as she shook it.

"I had no idea I'd be making that much money," Kaylee marveled.

"Don't get too excited," Sandra said. "Taxes eat up a lot. There's a lot of opportunity here. Make the most of it."

That was that. Kaylee was officially Alana's assistant.

For the next two hours, Alana walked Kaylee through the Teen Tower. As impressive as it was on paper, it was even more impressive in person. With opening day approaching, an army of men and women were hammering, welding, cleaning, and constructing. Alana showed Kaylee everything. The pool with its water-park features and forty-foot fountain. The faux casino where kids could "gamble" with free chips. The Teen Tower game room with dozens of screens and video games that could be played for free. The dining area that sat a thousand people comfortably. There was a state-of-the-art gym, virtual reality gaming area, movie theater, stage theater for live shows, and an outdoor stage and dance area with equipment for a deejay.

"The best part is that there's no money."

"How can that be?" Kaylee asked her as Alana walked her toward the visitors' check-in area.

"Simple. It's all-inclusive. No one who isn't on the guest list enters without a parent signing them in and showing ID. Then the parent pays a fee for each kid," Alana said. "A hundred fifty dollars a head for all day. When the kid is in, the kid is in. They can eat, play, do anything they want. No extra fees. No money needed."

"Kaylee! Wow! Hey, Alana! Hey!"

Alana turned. So did Kaylee. One of her father's personal trainers at the main hotel gym, Ellison, was striding across the pool deck toward them. He wore his training clothes from the gym and a pair of wraparound sunglasses. The sun gleamed off his powerful arms.

"Hey, guys," he greeted. "Alana, how're you doing? Kaylee, it's great to see you again. But what are you doing at Teen Tower?"

"I'm working here now," Kaylee told him. "I'm Alana's assistant."

He grinned. "Is that right? 'Cause I'll be working here too." He glanced at Alana. "Your dad just assigned me to the TT gym." He raised his eyebrows at Alana. "Hey. Can

I borrow Kaylee for a few? Show her around the gym? Maybe get an early lunch?"

Alana nodded, hoping that she looked innocent. It was no surprise that Ellison showed up when he did. She'd planned the whole thing and had actually asked her dad to put Ellison on the TT gym crew. She'd seen Ellison and Kaylee together at the party. Ellison seemed like a great guy. Kaylee didn't seem to have a boyfriend. She thought it would be cool to get Ellison and Kaylee together to see if they really liked each other. And this was a great time to do it, before Teen Tower opened and everyone got crazy busy.

"I think that'd be fine," Alana told them.

"Really?" Kaylee asked. "On my first day?"

Alana looked right at her. "Yes. On your first day. You work for me. If I say to go with Ellison, see the gym, and have some lunch, what you say in response is, 'Sounds good. I'll catch up with you later.' Got it?"

"Got it," Kaylee agreed readily. "Sounds good. I'll catch up with you later!"

CHAPTER TEN

By five o'clock on the afternoon of her first day with Kaylee, Alana had decided that working with her was the bomb.

For her whole life, Alana felt disconnected. Displaced. A disappointment, especially to her father. She was the girl who had everything but seemed to have accomplished nothing but looking cute. In school, she'd always been average. As an athlete, she was worthless. She was a decent but not great dancer, a decent but not great party-giver. She kept up a decent but not great Tumblr. She planned to apply to decent but not great colleges and expected to get into most of them, but suspected it would be because of the donation checks that the development offices hoped her father would someday send. She moved through life with a pretty face, great hair, the best clothes, and the finest jewelry money could buy ... and no confidence.

That is, until Kaylee Ryan came into her life. From that moment forward, everything changed.

When they met back up, Kaylee reported that during lunch, Ellison had suggested they drive out to Hoover Dam. Kaylee called it a "get-together." Alana determined, however, that it was a first date.

Kaylee also said she and Ellison had run into Chalice and Zoey. Alana was relieved to hear that her best friends had been their usual charming selves to Kaylee.

Now it was time to get back to work on Teen Tower. Alana and Kaylee started discussing ways to bring kids to Teen Tower not just for a single visit but for multiple times during the same week. Kaylee suggested something called the "Teen Time" pass, which would allow teens to visit for any three consecutive days that included a weekend for a slightly reduced fee. Alana thought it was a great idea since it might keep weekend visitors on the premises for an extra day. That would mean more revenue at the hotel and the casino as well as at Teen Tower. She couldn't wait to share the idea with her father. Kaylee had also come up with a cool concept for sports entertainment near the pool.

She had her chance late that afternoon when she and Kaylee met Steve and Roxanne at the Island Bar in the middle of the casino for a five o'clock debriefing. The Island Bar was one of her favorite places at the hotel. It had been decorated in a Caribbean theme with tropical plants flourishing and Calypso music playing. The wait staff were all from places like Barbados and Antigua. They served some of the tastiest alcoholic and non-alcoholic drinks in the city. It was separated from the rest of the casino by smoke-proof and sound-proof glass, so it really felt like an island.

Alana was the first to arrive for the meeting. The host seated her on a plush couch in the VIP area of the bar. Her father and Roxanne were next to arrive. Kaylee was oddly late, a fact that her father pointed out. Alana texted her to see what was going on. A moment later, Kaylee texted back.

"Broken heel. Getting glue. B there in 3 mins."

Alana laughed. "She broke her heel," she reported.

"Been there, done that more than once," Roxanne said sympathetically.

"How's she working out with you?" Steve asked after they ordered a round of drinks. He and Roxanne were having rum. Alana wanted a virgin piña colada. She ordered the same thing for Kaylee.

"She makes me want to do nothing *but* work," Alana reported once the drinks arrived. "I *love* working with her."

Steve beamed. "I love your attitude. That's the attitude it takes to make a success of yourself." He turned to Roxanne. "That's how I feel about you, you know. But not just about work, if you catch my drift."

Roxanne winked at him. Alana grimaced. Did her father realize how creepy it was to be so flirty in front of his daughter? Then she spotted Kaylee looking uncertainly around the Island Bar.

"She's here," she told her dad and Roxanne, waving at Kaylee. Kaylee beamed, waved sheepishly, then hurried over. The security guy opened the velvet rope to the VIP area, and Alana scooted over so Kaylee could join her on the couch.

Immediately, Kaylee started to apologize. "I'm so sorry I'm—"

"Late?" Roxanne asked. "Forget about it. You had a wardrobe malfunction. It happens to everyone."

"I got you a drink," Alana told her. "Virgin piña colada."

"That's perfect."

Steve grinned. "What's perfect is how Teen Tower is finally shaping up. Any other genius concepts Roxanne and I need to know about?"

Alana thought about the Teen Time pass. "Actually, yes, but not for the opening. For the business in general."

"Well, let's hear it." Steve was genuinely excited.

She told her dad and Roxanne about the Teen Time pass idea. They nodded with approval.

"So, what you're saying is, if a person buys the pass, they can tack on either a Friday or a Monday and extend the weekend," Roxanne surmised.

Kaylee spoke up. "Exactly. And the thing is, most people won't be there for the whole third day. They'll either be arriving or departing."

"So the reduced cost is offset by reduced expenses," Steve deduced. "Makes a lot of sense to me. Let's do it. Anything else?"

Alana nodded. "One more thing. We've got lots of room by the pool. Why don't we put in a couple of beach volleyball courts?" She looked at Kaylee, indicating that she should present the rest of the sports entertainment idea.

"What we were thinking," Kaylee said, "was a national beach volleyball challenge that would finish here at Teen Tower."

"In bikinis!" Steve exclaimed.

"With big prize money," Roxanne chimed in.

"And those two girls from the Olympics as the hosts," Alana added.

Steve nodded. "I like it. Let's talk to ESPN about

televising the finals. And maybe do MMA sometime too."
He sipped from his drink. "Anything else, girls?"

Alana shook her head. That covered everything. To her
surprise, Kaylee had one more thing to say.

"There's an idea about Teen Casino."

What idea about Teen Casino? She and Kaylee hadn't
talked about Teen Casino.

"Out with it," Steve encouraged.

Kaylee addressed Steve and Roxanne. "We think some
of the table games should be wheelchair accessible. And
others should be able to be played even if a person is
blind or deaf. When we say we're handicap friendly and
disability friendly, we really need to be friendly. Not every
table, just some of them. It'll be great publicity, and who
knows? Maybe it'll make some kid happy."

"And a happy kid is a happy parent, and a happy parent
is a happy guest, and a happy guest comes back," Roxanne
said approvingly, and then turned to Steve. "I think that's
a must-do. And maybe we should look into it in the main
casino too."

"I agree," Alana chimed in, looking significantly in
Kaylee's direction. As much as she liked Kaylee, the girl
needed a lesson in how things got decided and presented.
It wasn't right to go over Alana's head. Ever. "I'm glad I
thought of it."

Her words had their intended effect. Steve exulted while Kaylee looked hurt.

"That's my genius daughter!" Steve exclaimed.

There would have to be a serious conversation with Kaylee, Alana decided. But this wasn't the time or place for it.

Then Steve stood. So did Roxanne, even though they'd only had about half of their drinks. "Good work, girls. Kaylee, can you give us a few moments with Alana? We'll see you tomorrow."

The girls stood too. "Have fun tonight," Alana told Kaylee.

"You doing anything special?"

Alana nodded. "Checking out some new spa with Zoey and Chalice over by the Palms."

Kaylee grinned. "Don't get too relaxed. Okay. See everyone tomorrow."

Alana watched her leave. They all sat down again.

"Smart girl," Steve commented when Kaylee was well out of earshot.

"I told you she's the best," Alana reminded them.

Steve frowned slightly. "What do you know about her, Alana?"

"You mean personally?" Alana asked. She remembered how guarded Kaylee was about her past and her own decision not to press too deeply for details. "Not so much. Not that it matters. Does it?"

Roxanne folded her arms. "It may not matter. Or it might matter a great deal. What if she's a spy for one of our competitors? Trump, maybe?"

Alana laughed. It was a preposterous idea. Spies didn't come up with the kind of great ideas that Kaylee had offered. "That's crazy."

"Maybe not." The worried look on Steve's face deepened. "I have to tell you, genius daughter of mine, there's practically nothing on her. No last residence, no high school graduation record, nothing but a California bank account and a Los Angeles phone number. Which leads me to think there's some stuff she's not telling me. Us."

Alana felt a shiver of panic. She remembered when Kaylee called her, the area code was from L.A. But she hadn't given it two thoughts, especially when Kaylee had turned out to be such a good assistant. "It doesn't matter. She's perfect for me. Don't you dare fire her."

Steve relaxed. "I'm not planning to fire her. But I need to know who she is, where she's from, and where she's going. And you, Alana? You're going to find it all out."

CHAPTER ELEVEN

Four hours later, Alana was in heaven. A lithe Japanese massage tech named Akara was walking gently on her back.

"Paradise," Chalice declared.

"More than paradise," Alana agreed. All three massage tables were hard against the walls of the bamboo-and-jasmine scented room. There was a long gun-metal balance rail attached to the wall for the techs as they did their back-walking, but the masseuses seemed so agile that the rail was hardly necessary. Each tech wore drawstring calf-length pants and a loose blue top.

"Life does have its privileges," Zoey murmured. She too was facedown.

The girls were visiting Nogizaka Hill, the new

Japanese-themed salon and spa that had opened next to the Palms Casino Hotel. All the major resorts had spas—the one at the LV Skye was world-renowned for its spectacular level of pampering. Zoey's moms, though, had gotten a tip that Nogizaka Hill offered an authentic Japanese experience. They had sent their daughter and her friends to investigate. If the girls made a good report, the moms might write up the spa on their blog in a way that guaranteed its future success. If the girls came back negative, the moms could put it out of business with one blog posting. Such was the power of their keyboards.

Akara stopped her trek to work on one tight spot near Alana's left shoulder blade. It felt wonderful. At the same time, though, Alana realized that at some point she needed to sit down with Stacy and Sunshine, Zoey's parents, to talk about Teen Tower. Maybe she would invite them to lunch with her and her dad. Maybe Kaylee could even join them.

Akara stepped off her back, then moved lightly to the side of the table. The masseuses atop Chalice and Zoey did the same thing.

"Massage done. Now tea time," Akara said. "Come to the next room for tea, then shower, body scrub, shower, and baths. Much more to do. You have two hours more. You like?"

95

Alana nodded as the three masseuses found them colorful kimonos. "Yes. I like. A lot."

"Good." Akara presented Alana with a red kimono. "This is for you to wear. We'll bring tea now. You go through door, turn left to tea room."

The three Japanese women formed a neat line and then silently made their way out.

"What do you think so far?" Zoey asked her friends.

"Ten," Chalice answered.

They moved out of the massage room, their kimonos swishing, down a short hallway and made a left into the tea room. The room was octagonal with cushions scattered on the floor, *moko hanga* art prints on the wall, and a dual-vase *ikebana* flower arrangement on a black-and-white pedestal. There was also music. This was not surprising, but Alana hadn't expected the music to be performed live by an old Japanese woman playing a strange stringed instrument.

The three of them settled down on the cushions cross-legged. Once they were in position, Akara and the other techs entered and performed an elaborate tea service, pouring tea into traditional bowls. Then Akara told them she would return in a half hour.

"You enjoy the tea. Relax," she said before she bowed and departed.

"Ten," Chalice repeated. "Maybe even eleven."

"You can't go higher than ten," Zoey told her sourly. "You're breaking your own rules."

Chalice tasted the tea. "Twelve. They're my rules. I can make 'em and break 'em how I want."

"Speaking of break 'em," Zoey said. "Have you talked to Cory since the party, Alana?"

Alana shook her head. Despite Kaylee's urgings, she hadn't. The idea of a yak with Cory was just too painful. He'd made his intentions clear with his actions. She tasted her tea. Slightly sweet with notes of spice unfolding the longer she kept it in her mouth. The tea was as good as any conversation with Cory would suck.

"No. And I didn't actually talk to him at my party. He didn't say a word to me, remember?"

"Well, I ran into him at the Beamer dealership. I was bringing my car in, he was taking his out. He asked about you," Zoey went on.

"What?" Alana nearly spilled her tea. A little flutter rose in her heart.

"He actually asked about you twice," Chalice declared triumphantly.

Alana raised her eyebrows at her friend. "You were there too?"

Chalice shook her head. "Secondhand. From Zoey."

"But accurate," Zoey acknowledged. Then she frowned. "I'm telling you, there was something off about him. You should call him, Alana."

"After how he treated me at my party? Don't think so. He should call me."

"Don't be petty." Zoey stretched out her long legs and then crossed them. "They should serve sake here too. Premium sake. I'd love some."

Alana looked over at the musician. If she spoke English or was listening to their conversation, she gave no indication. Meanwhile, Alana's brain reeled with this news about Cory. Could she believe it? And if she did believe it, where did that leave her?

"That's not the reaction we were expecting," Chalice declared. "We thought you'd be happy. You know, all the available girls are gonna want to hook up with him this summer now that you don't seem interested. I wonder who he'll pick. It's gonna be a feeding frenzy."

"Chalice ..." Zoey warned, her voice low.

"Well, it's true. Let's be rational about it. On the hotness scale, he's a ten. I bet he'd be a ten in bed too. And he goes to college. All girls our age want to hook up with college guys," Chalice said bluntly. "So why not?"

Whoa. Alana didn't think that way. In fact, she was

still a virgin. She wasn't committed to being a virgin. If Cory were her boyfriend again, she doubted she'd stay a virgin for very long. But the idea of hookups left her cold. She often wondered whether the hookup culture made it harder for girls to find boyfriends. Like, if a guy could be with a different girl every month, why would he ever want to commit? No. Hooking up was not her, and it would never be her.

Zoey dead-eyed Chalice. "Chalice, I'm giving you an order. Stop talking about this. And don't start anything. Let Alana talk to him. That is, if she has the guts."

"Okay," Chalice readily agreed. "But only because I'm a nice person and Alana is our friend."

"Swear it," Zoey demanded.

Chalice held up one of her small hands. "I swear."

"Good. Glad that's settled." Then Zoey refocused on Alana. "How's it working out with the new assistant?"

"Omigod, she's so great—" Alana began, until Zoey cut her off with a wave of her hand. "What?"

Zoey sipped her tea before she spoke. "You need to check her out. Who she is, where she's from, what she knows, who she knows. Like that."

Alana startled. This was the same thing her father had said to her. "Why?"

JEFF GOTTESFELD

"Because I'm always looking out for my friends," Zoey told her. "So I did some looking. No Facebook, no Twitter account, no Tumblr, no Reddit, no nothing."

"Maybe she hates social media," Alana reasoned.

"Come on. Every girl with an actual pulse has at least one of those things. She's hiding something from you. What you don't know can hurt you, you know."

"We saw her at lunch today with that dude from the party," Chalice said helpfully. "Ellison."

"I know. He likes her. I made that happen," Alana told them.

"Know what she told us? She said that before she came out to Vegas, she'd worked as a nanny. A nanny. Are you kidding?" Zoey's voice dripped skepticism.

"Okay, I got it," Alana acknowledged quietly.

She felt awful. First the conversation with her dad and Roxanne about Kaylee. Now this from Zoey. It wasn't like Zoey had learned something that Alana couldn't have learned from a conversation with Kaylee. Plus, it would have been the easiest thing to Google her new assistant. The problem was, once someone gets Googled and something gets learned, then the person doing the looking has to deal with the information. What Alana didn't know hadn't hurt her so far. But she had to admit that her dad and Zoey were right. What she didn't know could hurt her someday.

There would need to be a talk with Kaylee sooner rather than later. Alana needed answers.

"Then do something about it," Zoey counseled.

Alana nodded. "Okay. I will. Now, can we just relax and enjoy the spa?"

She did try to enjoy it. She loved the body scrub and the shower, and the women-only baths. But she was worried too. About what would happen if she actually talked to Cory. And especially about what would happen when she talked to Kaylee.

Alana and her friends left Nogizaka Hill around ten thirty. All of them gave the spa glowing reviews. Zoey's mothers would get a fabulous report. As they headed for their vehicles—the spa didn't have a valet, which was kind of a zit on its flawlessness—the three of them saw a crowd gathering on the sidewalk between the spa and the Palms.

"What's going on?" Alana asked.

"Dunno, let's go see," Zoey said.

They hustled over and joined the big ring of people. In the center was a guy dressed in black clothes, a black duster coat, and a white mask. He was in the middle of a street magic act. He started by juggling knives after proving their sharpness by slicing effortlessly through sheets of papers. As part of his act, he bounced the lethal knives off his feet, thighs, forearms, and even his head, as though they were no more dangerous than a beach ball. Alana had never seen anyone do that before; she cheered along with the crowd. Zoey, meanwhile, started filming on her iPhone.

"Who is this guy?" Alana asked no one in particular.

One of the spectators, a woman in her twenties with dark hair in a bob and a short silver dress, turned to Alana. "He won't say his real name. Calls himself 'Phantom.' Isn't that great?"

He was great. The routine with the knives was death-defying. Phantom did one of the best illusions Alana had ever seen. He opened his briefcase and took out a clear plastic water bottle, then passed that bottle around the crowd so everyone could see it was filled with some clear liquid. When everyone was satisfied, he opened the bottle and poured half of the contents onto a child's plastic doll that he'd dropped on the sidewalk.

The doll shriveled up and smoke rose out of it. The crowd shivered and oohed. The liquid was obviously some kind of powerful acid.

Then Phantom smiled and told the crowd, "To your health!"

Then he put the bottle to his lips and swigged, long and hard.

Screams rose from the audience, louder and louder. Alana found herself believing that the guy was going to die. As she looked around, it was obvious that everyone else did too. But Phantom didn't die. Instead, he wiped his lips with his sleeve and grinned.

"How'd you do that?" someone called.

"Do what? This?" He took the bottle and turned it over again. Whatever was left in it streamed down onto the withered doll, which smoked and withered some more.

The crowd cheered and burst into applause. Phantom picked up the shriveled doll, put it and the bottle in his magician's bag, and jogged away. He never gave his real name or touted the name of the club where Alana was sure he was a performer. He didn't even pass a hat for donations.

"That was fantastic!" Chalice exclaimed. "Ten!"

"I wish I knew who he was," Alana muttered. "He could be great for Teen Tower."

Zoey tapped her iPhone. "Is that so? Because I've got the whole thing recorded. I'll show it to my moms. They'll probably write about it on their blog. By tomorrow? You and the whole town will know everything about him you

ever wanted to know, and probably some stuff you didn't."
She smiled. "Which is exactly what you should know
about Kaylee Ryan."

"Yeah on both counts," Alana agreed. She looked
forward to getting the low-down on this Phantom char-
acter. Maybe not so much about Kaylee.

CHAPTER TWELVE

The next morning at nine o'clock, Alana was back in Mondrian. She'd already read *Stripped*, where there was some coverage of Phantom from the night before, including Zoey's video. The moms, though, hadn't been able to find out anything about him and had actually posted a reward for information.

Mondrian was closed to the public, but that didn't mean that it was silent. Jeff Koons, the next artist in residence, was moving his work into the studio. The hotel provided professional art movers to help bring in paintings and sculptures in progress. At a quarter to nine, Steve had stopped by to check on his famous guest artist, and Alana had said hello. She was having a private breakfast here to start the day. When she said whom she was having breakfast with, Steve approved.

Now, though, she sat nervously. She was at a table for two outside the soundproof and bullet-proof glass that separated the studio from the restaurant proper. Already on the table were a carafe of mango juice, another of orange juice, a plate of freshly baked croissants, and a fruit platter. A waiter stood discreetly in the distance while a member of the hotel's security staff was at the locked entrance waiting for her guest to arrive. She'd dressed carefully for what she thought might be a difficult conversation—a maroon Zac Posen dress that flared wide at the thighs and rested loosely on her shoulders.

There he was. She saw him on the other side of the glass door.

Cory wore brown slacks and a tan, long-sleeve pull-over with the sleeves pulled up over his muscled forearms. He'd cut his hair since the night of the party; the shorter look made his chiseled features even more striking. As soon as he spotted Alana, he gave a friendly wave.

She stood to greet him, feeling all the same emotions she'd always had. It had been so hard for her to call him late the night before and invite him to breakfast. She would never have done it if Kaylee and Zoey hadn't both encouraged her. As he strode across the restaurant toward her, she easily recalled those golden months they'd had together during his senior year—her junior—when he always seemed to have an arm around her or her hand in his. And then the heartache of not hearing from him for months. She'd known intuitively not to chase him, especially after they'd decided not to try to do it long distance. It had been painful, though. So painful.

He took her in his arms. She hugged him and found the strength to brush her lips against his cheek. "Hi," he said. "I'm glad you called me."

"I'll let you know in a half hour if I feel the same way," she told him honestly.

He looked hurt for a split second, then rallied. "Fair enough. Shall we sit? This looks great. Who's coming into the studio? Jeff Koons, right? My mom and dad will have to come when they're back from Europe. They'll probably buy some art."

They sat. The waiter poured mango juice for Alana and a coffee for Cory. Alana wanted to get right to the main topic—his relationship with her, and especially how he'd been such a jerk to her at her birthday party. But she didn't have the guts.

"How's your family?" she asked instead.

He sipped his coffee and broke off a piece of croissant to eat before he responded. "Everybody's okay. It's going to be a typical summer. My mom went home to England. My father's with his parents in Greece. My brother's at tennis camp, then he's going to basketball camp, and then to Greece. My sister's in Los Angeles trying to get famous and succeeding a little. That never changes. I'm here."

"And what are you doing for the summer?" Alana asked, still stalling.

"Well … I'm trying to do my reading for next semester," he confessed. "I didn't exactly have a rockin' freshman year."

Alana raised her eyebrows. That was news. Cory had been at the top of his high school class. That's one of the reasons that Stanford had taken him. Having a father who was one of the most talented stock market gurus in the country didn't hurt either. The Las Vegas-based Philanopoulos Fund consistently outperformed just about every other hedge fund in existence.

She reached for a slice of golden peach, cut it daintily in half, and ate it, making sure not to dribble juice down the front of her dress. "Define, 'not exactly rockin'.' "

He peered at her. "You really want to know?"

"I really want to know, yeah."

He seemed to sigh. "Fine. Okay. I had a really hard time. In a lot of ways."

Cory had always been the golden boy of Las Vegas.

The idea of him having a hard time at anything was as likely as the idea that Alana's own father would suddenly ditch the hotel business in favor of digging ditches.

"How hard?"

"How does academic probation sound?"

She stared at him. "You're kidding."

"About that kind of thing I don't kid," Cory confessed. "I barely survived. My first semester grades were a disaster. Second semester wasn't better, not till the very end. Don't stare at me like that, I wasn't well."

Her heart beat heavily as a wave of sympathy overtook her. "You got sick? So you had to miss classes? I know kids that has happened to. It sucks."

He shook his head. "Nope. Nothing like that. Nothing wrong with my body. More like here." He tapped his head with his right forefinger.

"Omigod. You had a brain infection? From when you went mountain climbing with your dad in Peru?" Alana was shocked. She'd paid enough attention in biology class to know that a brain infection was bad news. Regular medicines didn't go between the body and the brain. She couldn't believe she didn't know any of this about him. Had he been in the hospital? She'd seen Cory's mom and dad at various charity functions over the last year. They hadn't said a thing. Weird.

Cory laughed wanly. "I wish. I'm talking mentally. I was depressed beyond belief. Couldn't really get out of bed some days. I was a total wreck."

"Omigod," Alana exclaimed. She wanted to embrace him and protect him, but at the same time was baffled by what she was hearing. "What do you have to be depressed about? Your life is, like, perfect."

"That's just it. There was nothing to be depressed about. Which is why everyone thought I was going to snap out of it. I didn't. Finally they sent me to psych services. The shrink taught me about stuff like serotonin and dopamine, and put me on an SSRI."

"Like Prozac?" Alana asked.

"Something like that. Same family of drugs. It took quite a while to find one that worked. Hold on. I've got to have another croissant."

He reached for another of the flaky, freshly baked croissants, then stopped.

"I need to apologize for something," he told her.

She raised her eyebrows, hoping …

For once, hopes were answered.

"I was a jerk at your party," he confessed quietly. "Once I hadn't called you from school and all the bad stuff happened, I didn't really know what to do. So when I got the party invite, of course I was going to come. But then, because I hadn't seen you … well, there were all these emotions. And I couldn't handle them."

"Thank you for telling me that," she murmured. "I felt bad."

"I felt bad too." He leaned forward and rested his head on his hands, elbows impolitely on the table. "Look. I'm not all myself yet. I'm better, but I'm not back. Honestly, I'm pretty fragile. I don't look fragile, and in some ways I don't feel fragile anymore. But I am. So … I'd like to be your friend again. You're about the only real person in this whole town. Let me know if that can happen. Okay. I'm going to eat this second croissant now."

With a big show, he bit into it. Alana grinned, and then she thought about all that Cory had shared with her. This was a lot of information, but it all actually made sense. He was the kind of guy who'd want to keep something like depression a secret. He hadn't done anything throughout the meal so far to give Alana the slightest indication that he wanted to get with her again *that way*, but Alana thought maybe things could change. She would need to take the long view. It might not happen right away. But maybe she could help it happen eventually.

She asked herself what Kaylee would do. And then she answered her own question with her words.

"Well," she said briskly. "I'm glad you're feeling better.

And I'm glad we're getting a chance to talk. Better here than at a party with a thousand of my dad's best friends."

"I'm glad you think that. Me too."

"All you're doing this summer is getting caught up on your reading?"

He nodded. "So far, yeah."

She smiled her most winning smile at him. "Well, I've got an idea that I think will work and still let you do all that reading. You know what I'm doing this summer, right?"

He nodded. "In charge of that Teen Tower thing."

"Exactly. And you know what? I think that you need to work with me on that project," she declared. "Starting right now."

CHAPTER THIRTEEN

Alana put Cory to work with the Teen Tower social media team. It took her about a half hour to take him through personnel, and another half hour to walk him to the bowels of the main hotel, where the social media center was located. There was a full-time staff of five in charge of the website, Twitter accounts, Tumblrs, Instagrams, and the like. Cory would work there on Teen Tower's social media presence until Teen Tower actually opened. Maybe longer. She'd find something else for him to do. He was thrilled. So was she.

Then it was time for her big talk with Kaylee. It was easier than Alana expected. Because Kaylee beat her to the punch. After a morning of working separately, they met for a catch-up lunch in the game room. Alana had

sandwiches ordered in from the main hotel kitchen—
brie and grilled shiitake mushrooms for herself, and two
barbecue free-range chicken wraps for Kaylee. Before
they started to eat, Alana asked Cory to stop by and introduce himself. Kaylee was soft-spoken and kind to him
and almost deferential to Alana. In Cory's presence, she
treated Alana more like her boss than like a friend. Alana
was impressed.

"I like him," Kaylee said when he was gone.

"Don't like him too much," Alana joked.

Kaylee raised her eyebrows. "Are you kidding? He's
your guy, only he doesn't know it yet. Anything I can do
to help, you let me know."

"Just keep doing what you're doing," Alana told her.
She unwrapped her sandwich and held it to her nose,
inhaling the aroma of the brie. "If only this wasn't a thousand calories."

"No kidding," Kaylee agreed. "I've gained five pounds
since I came to work for you."

Alana smiled and looked around the game room. It
was filled with pool, foosball, ping-pong, and other table
games, and ringed by dartboards. She wondered if it would
be possible to put in a few bowling alleys or if that would
be too noisy. Huh. That was the kind of thought that Kaylee
usually had. Maybe she really was getting good at this stuff.

"Has Ellison offered to train you yet? If he hasn't, I bet he will."

"And I might take him up on it," Kaylee confessed. "So. Here I am talking about weight with you. That's honest. Can I be honest about some other things?"

Alana felt her heart beat faster. Was Kaylee actually opening the door to a discussion that she knew they needed to have but had dreaded?

The answer was yes.

"Sure," she encouraged.

Kaylee seemed to blush. "I haven't talked a lot about myself because there's a lot about me that isn't really so great."

"It's going to take a lot to shock me," Alana assured her. "This is Vegas. Where people come to reinvent themselves, you know."

"Well, for example, I didn't really graduate from a regular high school. I was moving around too much. I did high school online. So if you ever Google me and try to see where I graduated, there's not really a record."

Alana peered at her. "Why'd you move around so much?"

"I was a nanny for this French family," Kaylee explained. "They lived a lot of places because of the dad's business. Texas mostly, for sure, but also Illinois and some

time in Arizona. So I did my schooling online that way."
She dug in her pocket and took out a folded sheet of paper.
"Here. This is the name of the family and their phone
number in Paris. If you need to call them, it's fine."

Holy wow. This was the last thing that Alana was
expecting. But it was exactly what she needed. She
couldn't wait to bring it to her father. And to show Zoey.
She knew it would put all these questions about Kaylee
to rest. Then everyone would accept her the way she was
supposed to be accepted.

But. There were two niggling things that still bothered
her.

"Your cell? Your bank account?"

"Excuse me?" Kaylee responded.

"Your cell phone. You have a California cell phone
number. But you said that you worked for this family in
Texas most of the time."

Kaylee smiled wanly. "They gave me the phone, and it
had a Cali number already. I don't know why. I'll change it
to Vegas if I need to for work. And they opened my account
for me in Los Angeles too. They travel a lot. I think they
do a lot of business with Wells Fargo or something."

Well. That made sense too.

"I'm glad you told me all this," Alana said. "I didn't

doubt you. In fact, unless you're an escaped felon, I could care less. But my dad ..."

Kaylee nodded. "I figured. Well, I hope we're good now."

Alana gave Kaylee's arm a squeeze. "We're good."

They were good for another ten hours. Just after eleven o'clock, Alana got two phone calls. One was from her father. The other was from Zoey. The calls made her do two things. First, go into her bathroom and throw up. Second, get in her car and drive to the Apache Motel.

CHAPTER FOURTEEN

You ready?" Zoey asked her as they stood outside room 109. It was Alana, Zoey, and Zoey's two moms, Stacy and Sunshine Gold-Blum. Alana knew they'd come because what was about to happen in Kaylee's room could be a major Vegas scandal that they would or could cover in *Stripped*.

The only saving grace was that Steve had decided not to come. Not because he thought it would be easier for Alana to confront Kaylee if she was alone, but because he thought it would be harder. When he called Alana with the news that Kaylee's stories about herself had completely unraveled, he hadn't tried to turn it into a teachable moment. He had been too angry. Instead, he ordered Alana to go and confront the girl and report to him in the morning.

"Knock," Stacy told her. Of the two moms, she was the taller and prettier one. Her partner, Sunshine, was crazy smart and a great reporter but looked like a Sonic Hedgehog.

Alana knocked. Kaylee answered a moment later. She wore jeans and a T-shirt. Alana watched her face turn white at the sight of the four people on her doorstep at this hour of the night.

"Supergirl! Meet my moms," Zoey said with a sneer.

"I know why you're here," she said softly.

Alana had trouble forming words. "Let. Us. In. Now."

Zoey stepped inside first and grimaced. "What a dump!"

Alana couldn't take her friend making this situation worse than it was. She hated what she was about to do. Hated, hated, hated it. In fact, she had real doubts whether it was even necessary. But after hearing from her father and from Zoey and her moms, she felt like there wasn't much choice. She had very little power.

"Everyone, sit down," Stacy ordered. "I'm Stacy Gold," she introduced herself to Kaylee.

"And I'm Sunshine Blum."

Alana moved to sit on the bed, where Kaylee had sagged onto the puke-green comforter.

"You might want to put a towel down before you put your butt there," Zoey cracked.

Alana tried to ignore Zoey. As bad as she thought seeing Kaylee would actually be, this was ten times worse. The girl was living here and keeping it a secret? Alana didn't find that deceitful. She found it remarkable. She must not have wanted Alana—and especially Steve—to judge her on the basis of appearances. If only she'd told the truth from the start. Alana would have gone through walls to protect her. After all, Kaylee had gone into a Champagne fountain to protect Alana.

"Is why you're here the reason that I think you're here?" Kaylee asked.

That was it. It was too much. Alana started to cry. Once she started, she couldn't stop. She was as bereft as when her mother had the nervous breakdown and couldn't even recognize her; couldn't even come up with her name.

Somehow, she found some words. They were harsher and more emotional than she intended. "How could you? How could you! How could you do this to me! I trusted you! Do you know what your lies did to me? All you had to do was tell the truth! The whole truth! Do you know what an idiot this makes me feel like?"

She cried some more. Tears streaked down her face and fell onto the simple white blouse she'd put on with her jeans.

"I'm sorry. I'm so sorry," Kaylee muttered, her eyes on the floor.

Zoey looked caustic. "Look what you've done to my friend. You've wrecked her, you've wrecked everything!"

"I said I was sorry!"

Stacy jumped in to the discussion. Her voice was calm and reasonable. Her words, though, were very scary. She'd said a variation of it to Alana when they'd met a few minutes before. Now, though, here in Kaylee's room, the words had extra weight.

"I don't think 'I'm sorry' cuts it here. Do you understand that there are hundreds of millions of dollars at stake? Teen Tower is about to open. Do you understand that every writer and blogger in the country is looking for a way to take Steve Skye down? His daughter and our daughter are best friends, that's true. But I think Steve is a conceited jerk," she declared matter-of-factly. "Everyone does, but no one can touch him."

Sunshine chimed in. "Don't you see, Kaylee? You've given us the way to touch him. We're itching to write about you and Alana and him. We've got an exclusive interview with you—it's happening right now. We can wreck him."

Stacy nodded. "The only reason we haven't uploaded the story is out of respect for Alana and Zoey's friendship and because we want to hear what you have to say. So, talk."

Kaylee looked toward Alana. "What do you know? What do they know?"

Alana shook her head and felt the tears come again. Ashamed of her own emotion, she hid her face in her hands. She could see the future so easily. No Kaylee in her life, which meant no muse for Teen Tower, and no person whose judgment she could trust. Kaylee had been the first one to urge her to contact Cory, no matter how painful it would be. It was exactly the right advice too.

Zoey spoke up. "We know everything. So does Steve Skye. We know about your mother and your aunt and your father. That you never finished high school, and that you're living at this dump. That you lucked into the catering gig, and that you were never a nanny. Never, ever, ever."

"Why didn't you just tell the truth?" Alana moaned. At least the tears had stopped for a few moments, though her face felt ravaged.

"I really am sorry, Alana," Kaylee told her.

Alana nodded slowly. She wanted to believe her friend's expression of remorse. Part of her even understood why her friend might lie. But part of her was just so angry that Kaylee had destroyed something beautiful. "I'd like to believe you, Kaylee. I would. But you don't exactly have a track record in the truth department, you know."

Kaylee turned toward the moms. "What can I do to stop you from writing about Alana and me? You haven't written anything yet, right?"

"Nope," Sunshine acknowledged. "Not yet."

"So. What can I do?"

Alana spoke up. What she was about to say were the hardest words she'd ever spoken. But considering what the stakes were, there was no real choice but to say them. "You need to leave, Kaylee. You need to leave town as soon as you can and not come back. I don't care where you go; no one does. Just don't come back to Vegas, and never talk about working with me."

"If you do that," Sunshine told her, "we won't write about you and Alana. Otherwise ..."

"Otherwise someone else is going to beat us to it. And we can't let that happen. If you leave, there's no story. If you stick around ..." Stacy's voice faded like a contrail in the sky on a breezy day.

Kaylee did not hesitate. "Okay. I'm gone in the morning," she declared.

And that was that. Alana, Zoey, and the mothers did not stick around for a post-mortem. Alana took one last look at Kaylee as she left the room. She imagined that she would probably never see this girl ever again.

CHAPTER FIFTEEN

Without Kaylee, Alana felt lost. The morning after the sad meeting at the motel, she wandered around the Teen Tower complex like a ghost, going through the motions as best she could. But she had nothing of any value to offer to anyone and could barely answer even the simplest question. When workmen asked her whether she wanted another coat of silver paint on the interior of the girl's pool bathroom stalls, she had no response. She told them to do what they wanted and fled to the quiet of the gym. There, she settled down on one of the blue crunch mats and tried to pull herself together. She told herself she had no options; Kaylee had lied to her and her father, and a hatchet job in the *Stripped* blog would be a disaster.

"Hey, Alana."

Alana looked up. Ellison was standing beside her. He dropped gracefully to his haunches and squatted next to her.

"Hey," she muttered.

"Where's your shadow?" he asked.

"My ...?"

"Shadow. Assistant. The beautiful and mysterious Katherine Ryan," he said. "Where Alana is, Kaylee is."

"Not anymore. She's gone," Alana said softly.

"No way. What happened?"

"Long story short," Alana said. "She couldn't pass a background check."

"She's been to *jail*?"

Alana shook her head. "Nah. Nothing like that. She just didn't tell us the truth about some things. You know my dad. If you're not straight with him ..." She made the shape of a gun with her forefinger and thumb and pulled the trigger. "*Adios*."

"That's too bad. I liked her. We went out to Hoover Dam, you know," Ellison said. "A couple of nights ago."

"I know. She told me." Alana sat up and wrapped her arms around her knees.

He looked pensive. "She didn't say much about herself. I guess I understand why now."

"You want to know her real deal?" Alana offered.

Ellison sat down and stretched out his legs. He sighed. "No, actually. I don't. If she wanted to tell me, she would tell me. Other than that, it's kinda none of my business if—"

"Hey! Alana! What are you doing?"

Alana froze. Her father. He stood at the entrance to the gym, hands on hips. With him was Roxanne.

Alana scrambled to her feet. "I'm outta here."

"Good luck," Ellison told her.

"This is not a time to flirt with the help," her father exclaimed when she reached him.

"I wasn't flirting."

Roxanne laughed sourly. "That's not what it looked like to us."

Alana glared at her. "Maybe you need glasses, then."

Roxanne's eyes widened. "Being rude does not become you, Alana."

Steve folded his arms. "I think I know what's really going on here. I'm going to ask you something, Alana, and I want an honest answer. Do not even think of lying to me. Do you agree with my decision to get that girl out of our lives?"

Crap. That was the last question Alana wanted to answer. She'd thought about it from the moment her father had told her that Kaylee had to go. She'd thought about it in Kaylee's motel room. She'd mused on it after the deed was done. She was still thinking about it. She had never met anyone like Kaylee, and now she was gone. Kaylee had said that she wished she would have just told the truth from the start.

She faced her father head-on. "I'd take her back in a heartbeat. She was the best assistant any girl—or guy—could want."

"Thank you for not lying," Steve said. "At least you didn't lie to me." He turned to Roxanne. "You're in charge of Teen Tower until my daughter gets her head screwed on straight again. Alana, your job is to show up, look cute, act like you're in charge even though you aren't, and keep your mouth shut. Come on, Roxanne. Let's go."

Alana was stunned. After everything she'd done—okay, with Kaylee's help, but still—she'd just been taken off the project.

Her dad and Roxanne walked away toward the pool area.

"Hey," Alana called. "Hey! You can't just dump me like that."

Then she realized that not only could they dump her, they just did.

CHAPTER SIXTEEN

The next afternoon, Alana sat with Cory out by the Teen Tower pool under the waning Vegas sun. Gentle misters cooled them. It was hard to believe that tomorrow this area would be packed with happy kids. Four thousand advanced tickets had already been purchased. Add to that a guest list of a few hundred and Teen Tower would be approaching its forty-five hundred person capacity.

Everything was set for the opening, though Alana's role had been reduced to that of a powerless puppet in a designer dress and gorgeous shoes. There had been staff meetings, security meetings, entertainment meetings, food service meetings, communications meetings, and safety meetings. The opening day menu would be the one that Alana and Kaylee had suggested. The Olympic volleyball players were set to do a special exhibition at noon, and the divers right afterward. Kid Cudi and the Detroit-based artist Tone Def would perform at three. It would be streamed on the Teen Tower website that Cory had helped with and taped for later broadcast on MTV. Cory had been working nonstop on a social media presence that had already attracted kudos from the *Stripped* blog. The Teen Tower Twitter feed already had one hundred thousand followers. People were reserving days well into the future.

"How much is four thousand times a hundred fifty?" Alana asked Cory. They were stretched out on adjoining silver chaise lounges with built-in pillows. Alana had the staff bring out a bottle of the special LV Skye no-alcohol "Champagne" her father had bottled for Teen Tower. She'd poured flutes for herself and Cory. They'd finished one glass and were working on their second.

"Six hundred thousand," Cory answered. "You know that."

"I do, but I'm making a point. You know what a money machine this place is going to be? Six hundred thousand times three hundred sixty-five days is two hundred nine-teen million dollars. My dad does it again," Alana said. "If only he wasn't such a jerk. He could have stood up to the moms about Kaylee, you know. They hate him, but they need him too."

"I think that's true. I think your dad wanted your assistant out of here. She scared him somehow."

"That's hard to believe," Alana murmured.

Cory sipped his drink. "Believe it. And believe that he was looking for a way to put Roxanne in charge too."

Alana paled. "You think?"

Cory nodded. "Look at the end result. He gets to parade you around as the young talent, and his new girlfriend thinks that he's given her all the power. It's perfect for them both."

Alana literally had not considered that as a possible reason for what had happened with Kaylee and her. It was so … well, it was almost evil, she decided.

"Kaylee and I could have done the job, you know," she told Cory.

"I know."

It was so great being with him. That he was her friend again meant the world to her. In fact, if it wasn't for his friendship, she didn't know how she'd have gotten through the days since Kaylee left. All Kaylee had done was do her job and do it well. She hadn't asked for anything from her except jobs for a couple of her friends. Alana felt a sudden pang of regret that she hadn't moved on that. Probably, though, those friends would have been fired too.

There was one thing that was still bothering her,

though. She hadn't told anyone that Kaylee was the one who'd come up with all the ideas about Teen Tower that Alana had taken credit for with her father. Not even Zoey and Chalice—especially not Zoey and Chalice. That would be too juicy. It would filter back to the moms, and she'd be reading about that in *Stripped* too.

Cory, though, had bared his soul to her. He'd told her the truth about something that no one else in Vegas knew. It wasn't fair that he would do that, and she wouldn't tell him her secret too.

"You know, Cory? All those great Teen Tower ideas? They weren't really my ideas," she said softly.

"Ha."

"I mean it. They weren't mine," she went on.

He sat up and looked at her. "Whose then? Your father's? He was giving you credit for them. I don't believe that."

Alana shook her head. "Nope. They were Kaylee's. She gave them to me, and I shared them with my dad. He still thinks they were mine. But they weren't."

"You're serious." He swung his legs around toward her and put a hand under his chin, contemplating the import of what she had just told him.

Alana nodded. "Totally. They weren't. She's the creative one. I'm, like, the lamest."

Cory laughed. It made Alana feel terrible.

"What's so funny?" she challenged. "I just told you something that no one else knows. Don't laugh at me."

Cory laughed harder. "Don't you get it, Alana? You're an idiot."

"I am not an idiot. I asked you to come out here because I'm having a really hard time. Thanks for nothing. Find your way out." She stood to leave, thinking she had totally misjudged him. How could he be so cruel as to laugh at her? Then to call her an idiot?

He stood too. "Don't go."

"Cory, you just called me an idiot."

His face grew soft. "Because you are. Tell me this: who decided that Kaylee should be your assistant?"

Alana thought back to the session with her father in the penthouse library. "Me."

"And who convinced the toughest man in America, namely, your father, that she should be your assistant?"

Alana fidgeted a little. "Me."

"And who worked with her and thought she was great, and gave her the room to speak her mind and let her imagination flow and come up with all these ideas?"

She fidgeted some more. She'd never thought of it like that. "Me, I guess."

"Alana, that's what a boss is supposed to do. You're a great boss, and I rest my case. Go home if you want. Or sit out here and drink faux Champagne with me. And thank you for listening. Most girls would have stomped away."

He sat again. So did she. He lifted his glass to her. "To a great boss."

She lifted her glass and her eyebrows. "To a great person. Who's doing a great job here too."

They clinked glasses and drank. His eyes caught hers.

"I like who you are," he said, his voice husky.

"I'm glad."

He leaned forward. They were inches apart. For him to kiss her, all he would have to do was lean forward and—

Her iPhone sounded. It was a text from the head of security for Teen Tower.

"Courier letter for you. Want me to hold it?"

She sighed.

"Work," she told Cory. "Gotta handle this, even if I have no power."

She texted back.

"No. Send it in. Am poolside."

Two minutes later, one of the hotel's uniformed security people—a middle-aged woman—came trotting up with a manila envelope.

"Who's it from?" Alana asked.

The woman shook her head. "No idea."

"Thank you," Alana told her.

The woman nodded and took off.

"What is it?" Cory asked.

"That's what we're going to find out." She tore open the seal and took out a handwritten letter.

"Holy crap," she muttered after the first sentence.

"What?" Cory asked.

"Hold on."

It didn't take Alana long to read it. Cory waited respectfully. Then she looked up at him.

"You're not gonna believe this," she reported. "It's from Kaylee. She's still in Vegas. And she has a plan for tomorrow that she wants me to help her with."

"What kind of plan?" Cory asked her.

Alana passed him the letter. "You won't believe it either unless you read it yourself."

Cory took the letter and read it quickly. When he was done, he looked up at her. "You going to do what she asks?"

Alana scanned the dim pool deck and got a faraway look in her eye. "I think it's going to be a Teen Tower opening that no one is *ever* going to forget."

CHAPTER SEVENTEEN

Alana knew. Cory knew. But no one else knew that Kaylee and some other people were coming to the Teen Tower opening. Alana didn't even tell Ellison. The fewer people who knew about it, the safer Kaylee would be. Steve, Roxanne, Zoey, and Chalice all knew Kaylee's face. If any of them had an inkling that Kaylee would be showing up, or if any of them caught a glimpse of her face before Kaylee did what she said in the note she was going to do, the consequences could be dire. No. Alana realized how important it was to do two things. First, sneak Kaylee safely onto the Teen Tower grounds. Second, do everything she could to keep her friend out of sight and out of everyone's mind.

It was not all that hard to engineer. Even though Alana

had no actual power, she did have a lot of access. One of the things she had access to was the VIP guest list. These were people who would be admitted simply by giving the security people their names. She added a few names to the guest list, including a made-up name for Kaylee, Julia Jones. Alana had no idea why Kaylee had chosen the name Julia, but it was as good as any. When she was done, the list was longer by three names. Since there were a few hundred people already listed, no one was the wiser for it.

In her note, Kaylee had made another suggestion that she thought would both help the Teen Tower opening and help the plan that Kaylee and her friends wanted to carry out. It wasn't mandatory, but it would be very useful for the purposes of misdirection. If the crowd's attention was focused in one direction, it would be easier for Kaylee and her friends to prepare what they wanted to do. Which is why, the night before the opening, Roxanne got a strange phone call from Alana. "I have an idea for the Teen Tower opening," Alana had said.

"Now?" Roxanne scoffed. "Now you have an idea? We open at ten in the morning. Save it."

Alana bore in. "Nope. You have to listen to me. It's great. Everyone will love it. And you—well, you've got connections; you can put it together in two hours. I know you can."

"Forget it. Pick your outfit for tomorrow and go to bed."

"Roxanne. Do you *really* want me to tell my dad that I had *a game-changing idea* for the Teen Tower opening, and you *didn't even want to hear it*? He won't be happy about that." Alana played her trump card.

There had been two beats of silence after that.

"Okay. Let's hear it."

"Okay. Fashion show on the pool deck. Mix of professional models and volunteer kids. Strutting the runway in swimsuits. Let the kids keep the swimsuits. And let my dad do his welcome message from the runway." The words tumbled out one after another as Alana presented Kaylee's idea.

There was more silence after that. Then Roxanne finally spoke.

"Okay. I get it. I'll make it happen. Your job will be to find the kids. See you tomorrow." Roxanne clicked off.

Alana punched the air with both fists. Mission accomplished.

By mid-morning the next day, the fashion show was in place. Alana didn't know how Roxanne had pulled it together and frankly didn't care. All she knew was that a T-runway had been erected on the pool deck, and a bunch of models and clothes had been flown in from

Los Angeles. Zoey and Chalice had arrived before Teen
Tower official opening time. Alana enlisted them not only
as fashion show models but also to help gather the girls
and guys who would be the volunteer models. Zoey and
Chalice took their jobs very seriously, which was just fine
with Alana. The more time they spent finding models, the
less time they would have to possibly spot Kaylee. As for
Kaylee, Alana checked the guest list at eleven. The name
Julia Jones had been crossed off by the security people.

Kaylee was in.

The Teen Tower opening was fantastic. Alana and Cory
wandered around together taking it all in. He wore red
surfer jams and a white T-shirt; she had on a sleek, jet black
skirt and a cut-off top that bared her midriff. The food area
was rollicking and happy. Kids were chowing down on
Kobe beef burgers, pastured chicken barbecue, über high-
end Mexican, and the best pizza they'd ever tasted. Kerri
Walsh Jennings and Misty May-Treanor played a beach
volleyball exhibition, followed by the divers from the US
Olympic team. The no-money casino was as crowded
and exciting as the main hotel casino. Kids were lined
up three-deep around all the table games. The gym, the
virtual reality game room—everything was happening. A
deejay spun out by the pool deck; kids danced in front of
the performance stage. Workers were making last-minute

adjustments to the fashion T-runway, putting up the blue curtains behind which all the models would dress.

At about two o'clock, not long before the fashion show was supposed to start, Alana went to the dining room and filled a plate with food. Then she discreetly made her way up a secured rear staircase to the second level of Teen Tower; the level used mainly for storage and deliveries. She was alone. No one knew her mission. Following Kaylee's instructions from the note, she moved down a corridor to a storage room on the west side, next to a balcony that looked out over the pool deck. Then she gave three hard knocks to the storage room door.

Knock-knock-knock.

The door opened. There was Kaylee in black jeans and a black T-shirt.

"Hi, 'Julia.' I thought you might be hungry."

Kaylee seemed not to be able to find words as Alana put the plate of food on a shelf. Then the two girls hugged like they hadn't seen each other in years instead of it being just a few days.

"Omigod, omigod, I'm so glad you're here. I'm so glad you didn't leave town! Thank you, thank you, thank you," Alana told her.

"No. Thank you for understanding. How's your dad treating you?" Kaylee asked.

Alana shrugged. "Like my dad. What do you expect?"

"Well, when this afternoon is over, he's going to think you're the greatest thing to hit Vegas since the slot machine," her friend promised.

"I can't stay up here for long," Alana said.

"You don't have to," Kaylee assured her. "I can see everything."

"What's going to happen tomorrow? When all this is over?" Alana wondered aloud. She hoped that if their plan was successful, her father would insist that Kaylee come back to work at Teen Tower. But maybe he wouldn't. Maybe he'd be furious anyway. There was still so much that was out of her control.

"Dunno. You're the boss."

Alana grinned and looked out the storage room window. She could see lots of activity on the T-runway. "Yeah, I guess I am. Okay, show's about to start."

"You picked out the peeps you want? Are there enough? Anyone say no?"

"To wear designer suits that they can keep and have four thousand people cheering for them? Are you crazy? I got forty."

"That should be enough."

"Okay. I'm outta here. Eat up. The food is fantastic! You're the best, Kaylee. *Thank you.*"

She hugged her friend one more time, then slipped out of the storage room, hustled down the corridor, and took the same stairway to the pool deck. Then she hurried behind the blue curtain where dozens of models and dressers were prepping for the show that would start in just a few minutes.

"Where've you been?" Zoey challenged. She was ready for the show, wearing a gorgeous Rodarte dress. The plan was for the models to remove these outfits, revealing the gorgeous swimsuits they'd be wearing underneath.

"I got held up, okay? Lemme get dressed!"

Alana stepped away; she knew there were only a few moments until the show began. As she put on her bikini, her father stepped out onto the fashion runway with a handheld microphone. Since there were monitors in the dressing area, she could see his whole welcoming speech. After he revved up the crowd, he started the show.

"Thanks to the wonderful Roxanne Hunter-Gibson, who just this morning brought in some model friends from L.A., and especially thanks to my brilliant daughter, Alana Skye, for the idea, and thanks to all of you who answered Alana's call to help out, here's a little something we call, *Swimming on the Strip!*"

Roxanne was the first model; she wore a black dress. At the end of the runway, she pulled at the neckline; the dress ripped away. Underneath was a sizzling black bikini. The crowd had no idea that the models would be removing their designer duds to reveal stunning swimwear. They roared their approval. There were more models—some of them professionals, some of them friends and kids from the crowd whom Alana, Zoey, and Chalice had picked out. Zoey stripped down to a black tank suit cut in the back nearly to her rear; Chalice was gorgeous in a tennis outfit that hid a gray bikini.

Then Alana stepped out in a long-sleeve white evening gown.

"Alana Skye!" her father shouted, introducing her.

Alana had never modeled, but she'd watched enough fashion shows to know what to do. She strutted to the end of the runway in her flowing Versace gown as the crowd cheered appreciatively. She pulled at the neckline; the Velcro on the modified gown opened to reveal her white nineteen twenties-style bathing costume. The crowd roared with laughter. Alana snuck a glance up toward the storage and balcony area hoping to spot Kaylee. But her friend was well hidden. Then she pulled at the neckline of the bathing costume; it broke away to show off a fantastic pink bikini.

The crowd cheered. Alana blew some kisses and waved, then strutted back to the dressing area. All she could do now was wait for the fashion show to end, then the rest of Kaylee's plan was supposed to unfold. She was excited, but she was also frightened. If the plan worked, it would be genius. If it failed, Alana would be humiliated, and the Teen Tower opening would be ruined. It simply could not fail.

As the show unwound, Alana got more and more nervous. Fortunately, Cory came backstage to join her.

"Stay cool," he suggested.

"Uh-huh. Good luck to me."

"Come on." He took her by the elbow. "Let's go out and watch."

Alana shook her head. "Can't. I'm in the big finale."

"Then meet me by the lifeguard stand afterward," Cory told her.

"If I can."

The show finally ended. All the models, Alana included, went down the runway together in their swimsuits. They waved to the crowd and basked in the applause and cheers. Alana could barely focus, though. At any moment—

"Hello, hello!" Kaylee's voice reverberated throughout the pool deck. "Up here! Hey! Up here!"

Everywhere, people pointed to a second floor balcony. There, Kaylee stood with a handheld mic.

Alana's breath caught in her chest. For better or worse,

this was it. She looked to her left. There stood her father and Roxanne, looking like they'd each been hit by a bulldozer. They stared as Kaylee kept up her enthusiastic patter. "Hello, Las Vegas! Hello, Teen Tower! I've got a special guest for you! Are you ready?"

The crowd buzzed as someone dressed in black stepped forward. Alana grinned—it was Phantom, the same magician whom she and her friends had seen do the fantastic illusion outside the spa by the Palms. Many of the people in the crowd seemed to have read the *Stripped* blog or had heard about Phantom's exploits, because people started pointing at the balcony and calling his name.

Alana watched Kaylee raise the mic to her mouth again. "Teen Tower, watch Phantom as he dazzles and amazes you!"

Then Phantom took the microphone. "I want to thank the great Alana Skye for inviting me. What Alana wants? Alana gets. Give it up for Alana!"

The crowd roared. All Alana could do was grin, though her stomach was twisted into knots. Alana had known those words were coming, but with them came finality. Whatever happened would be her responsibility. Then Kaylee pointed at Alana, who pointed back. The crowd thought she was pointing at Phantom, and they cheered again.

Then came the trick. It was an illusion that Vegas would be talking about for years.

Phantom started by wrapping a black cloak around Kaylee's head.

"Watch!" Phantom ordered. The crowd silenced itself so quickly that Alana could hear a jet take off from McCarran Airport miles away. Phantom let the tension build. Then he made a momentous announcement.

"And now, I give you, 'Phantom's Silent Woman!' "

He pulled the cloak away.

The crowd gasped.

For all the world, it somehow looked like Kaylee had lost her head. Her body stopped at the neck.

People screamed. Then they cheered at the magnificent illusion. Alana stared, trying to figure out how Phantom and Kaylee had done it. Then Phantom reversed the process, and Kaylee's head reappeared. The crowd roared.

"Thank you! Thank you, Alana! Thank you, Las Vegas. *Stripped* blog, you'll be hearing from me! Thank you again!" Phantom made a deep bow.

Alana knew what she had to do. This wasn't in the scenario that Kaylee had proposed in her note of the night before, but it was the theatrical thing to do. It was also the right thing to do.

She pushed over to the deejay stand and took one of his microphones.

"And thank you, Phantom and Kaylee Ryan!" She raised a hand to the balcony. "Ladies and gentlemen, Phantom and Kaylee!" Then she saluted Kaylee with an air fist-bump. Kaylee air fist-bumped her back. Then Phantom disappeared. Into thin air. The crowd was dead silent.

Everyone screamed and shouted with approval, chanting "Phantom, Phantom, Phantom" over and over again. The noise was deafening.

Behind the scenes, the plan was for Phantom to make a grand escape and for Kaylee to make a grand entrance. Alana wanted to greet her as she came down from the second level. What she hadn't counted on was that four thousand kids would want to greet her too. It was a crush of humanity all the way from the pool deck to the doors that led to the second level. The reunion was going to have to wait.

A discussion with her father, however, did not. Smiling at everyone like the idea for Phantom's performance had been his all along, he cornered Alana as she tried to get to Kaylee. He was alone. No Roxanne. The smile was the only thing pleasant about him.

"What the hell just happened?"

Alana raised her shoulders. "It was awesome, wasn't it? The crowd loved it." She cocked her head at him. "I bet it's gonna be on *Stripped* in about five minutes."

The fake smile never left her father's face. "I don't like surprises like that."

"Come on, Dad," Alana cajoled. "It was the best!"

"That girl was supposed to have left town. How long have you two been planning this?"

Alana looked past her father. Kaylee was talking with Ellison. If Alana could get away now, she could reach her before the crush began again.

"Dad? You have to excuse me. We can talk tomorrow. Promise. Have a great time today. It's a great day for the Skye family!"

With that, Alana stepped away from her dad, hoping that he wouldn't follow her. Fortunately, he didn't. And then she was behind Kaylee, who had separated from Ellison and seemed to be looking for someone.

She tapped Kaylee on the shoulder and said, "Looking for me?"

Kaylee turned around. A grin spread over her mouth. The girls gave each other a quick hug.

"Yeah," Kaylee told Alana. "Happy?"

"Ecstatic." Alana snapped her fingers. "Hey, I have an idea. Wanna be my assistant? I hear there's an opening."

Kaylee grimaced. "What about your dad?"

Alana thought about the conversation she'd just had with her father. It was the first time in her life that she'd really stood up to him. He hadn't backed down, but neither had she.

"I don't have to worry about Daddy," she said proudly.

Kaylee frowned. "You always have to worry about Daddy."

"Really?" Alana countered confidently. "I'm eighteen. Which means that if I want to hire you, I can do it on my own. No way he fires me after *this* opening. In fact, he *owes* me. Which means he owes you too. You in?"

She saw Kaylee's eyes fill with tears. It was touching.

"I'm in," Kaylee said softly.

"Work starts at eight tomorrow morning. Be early." Alana glanced around the pool deck. So many people were watching this conversation. Ellison and Cory. Zoey and Chalice. Her father and Roxanne. And so many others. She hoped they were witnessing the official start of something great. Not just at Teen Tower, but between herself and Kaylee Ryan.

"Can I start with a phone call?" Kaylee asked.

"To whom?"

Kaylee grinned. "Zoey's moms. I want *Stripped* to interview me."

Well then. There was only one reasonable response to that.

"Not without me on the line too," Alana declared. "Any other surprises for me today?"

"Nope. I've had enough for one day."

Alana smiled cagily. "Well, I've got one more for you."

Kaylee raised her eyebrows. "Dare I ask?"

"Where are you living these days? You left that fleabag motel."

"In North Las Vegas with some friends."

Alana shook her head. "Not anymore. Bring your suitcase in the morning. I'm putting you up here. Your own room. And I'm your boss, so don't even think about refusing."

Kaylee looked shocked. "Thank you."

"You're welcome." Alana realized it was time to wrap this up. Teen Tower was supposed to be about fun, not about work. Her job was to make sure people had a great time. She sold dreams for a living. "And have those two friends of yours call me tomorrow. I'll find work for them too."

"You remembered!" Kaylee exclaimed.

"Of course I remembered." Alana pointed to the pool. "I think we should go swimming."

"I didn't bring a suit."

"Don't let that stop you. I lent you clothes before, I'll do it again." Alana pointed to the water. "I'm your boss, and that's an order. In. Now. Together. One, two, three!"

They jumped; Alana in her bikini; Kaylee in the same clothes in which she'd performed with Phantom. They came up sputtering and happy. The applause from the Teen Tower guests who'd seen them take the plunge echoed in the desert heat.

"Welcome to your future," Alana told Kaylee as they treaded water side by side.

One by one, kids started jumping into the water around them. Jumping, diving, belly-flopping, cannon-balling, whooping and hollering as they flew through the air and splashed down, sending up great shimmering plumes of water. It was like water fireworks, and it was way cooler than any airborne fireworks that her father had set off at her eighteenth birthday party. Those had been given. These felt like they'd been earned.

"Thank God I'm here," Kaylee declared.

Full of life, and love, and fearless of whatever was coming next, Alana dived to the bottom of the pool, then pushed off the blue concrete and burst upward through the water, exploding out of the pool's surface like a rocket. It felt like being born again. Alana didn't know if it was God who brought Kaylee to Las Vegas. Or fate, or luck, or some strange Vegas-y combo of the three. It didn't really matter. What mattered was that Kaylee *was* there. She finally had someone watching her back who didn't have an agenda. And she'd helped Alana impress the unimpressable Steve Skye. None of her friends had ever done that.

It made Alana impatient for the next minute, the next hour ... she couldn't wait to go to work the next day.

For the first time in her life, everything felt possible.

JEFF GOTTESFELD

Jeff Gottesfeld is an award-winning writer for page, screen, and stage. His *Robinson's Hood* trilogy for Saddleback won the "IPPY" Silver Medal for multicultural fiction. He was part of the editorial team on *Juicy Central* and wrote the *Campus Confessions* series. He was Emmy-nominated for his work on the CBS daytime drama *The Young and the Restless*, and also wrote for *Smallville* and *As the World Turns*. His *Anne Frank and Me* (as himself) and *The A-List* series (as Zoey Dean) were NCSS and ALA award-winning *Los Angeles Times* and *New York Times* bestsellers. Coming soon is his first picture book, *The Tree in the Courtyard*. He was born in Manhattan, went to school in Maine, has lived in Tennessee and Utah, and now happily calls Los Angeles home. He speaks three languages and thinks all teens deserve to find the fun in great stories. Learn more at www.jeffgottesfeldwrites.com.

WANT A DIFFERENT
point of view?

JUST *flip* THE BOOK!

WANT A DIFFERENT
point of view?

JUST *flip* THE BOOK!